Our virtues and our failings are inseparable,
like force and matter.
When they separate, man is no more.

Nikola Tesla

Dave Stutler:

So, wait . . . is sorcery science or magic?

Balthazar Blake:

Yes.

THE ANSWER IS YES: THE ART AND MAKING OF

Disney

THE SORCERER'S APPRENTICE

Written by Michael Singer

Foreword by Jerry Bruckheimer / Afterword by Jon Turteltaub

A WELCOME BOOK

Disney
EDITIONS
NEW YORK

ELEMENTS

OPPOSITE: Assistant art director Gregory Hill's conceptual illustration of the Grimhold.

Foreword
Jerry Bruckheimer

Can there possibly be a better match than movies and magic?

After all, the two have now been associated with each other for considerably more than a century. The inventors of motion pictures were something like magicians themselves, conjuring up a new form of art and entertainment, pulling a brand-new rabbit from an even newer hat. And ever since, there have been pioneers who have used their vision and genius to continuously boot the media up to new levels.

It goes without saying that the movie legend most associated with magic is Walt Disney. In a startling show of insight, he saw the technology that he and his associates were constantly innovating on movie screens, then television, and finally in theme parks, not as an end in itself, but as a way to immerse and surround the public—the audience—with images, sound, and light never before experienced.

Almost ten years ago, I was handed a baton that had been passed down from the hands of the Great Man himself when I was asked to develop the Pirates of the Caribbean. It was the last Disney Theme Park ride in which Walt Disney had a personal hand in developing; he never lived to see Pirates of the Caribbean's debut and subsequent great success, not just as a ride, but also as a motion picture. It wasn't a task that I took lightly. We wanted to honor the basis of the ride but, at the same time, sought to unhinge those wonderful boats from their tracks, so to speak, and set them sailing in unknown directions. Three *Pirates of the Caribbean* movies later, with a fourth on the way, it's gratifying to know, based not only on box office but, more importantly, on the impact that the films seemed to have in popular culture, that we lived up to audiences' expectations and, hopefully, honored Mr. Disney and his vision in a suitable fashion.

And now, here we go again. Only this time, the foundation for our new epic of fun, fantasy, romance, and magic is not only one of the most venerated of all Walt Disney animated films, but also a story that goes back generations. From German poet Johann Wolfgang von Goethe in 1797, to French composer Paul Dukas in 1897, to Walt Disney's *Fantasia* in 1940, for over two hundred years "The Sorcerer's Apprentice" has, in its various incarnations, enchanted readers, music lovers, and animation aficionados with its timeless tale of runaway magic, and how one must learn to walk before the running can begin. In *Fantasia*, Walt Disney's greatest creation, Mickey Mouse, learns the hard way. In our new film, it's a college physics major named Dave Stutler. Dave steadfastly believes only in science until a sorcerer named Balthazar Blake unexpectedly enters his life and, in the ensuing adventures, proves that magic and science are not necessarily incompatible. "Everything we do is well within the laws of physics," says Balthazar to an as-yet disbelieving Dave. "You just don't know all the laws yet."

With our marvelous cast led by Nicolas Cage, Jay Baruchel, Alfred Molina, Teresa Palmer, Monica Bellucci, and Toby Kebbell, and the brilliant Jon Turteltaub—who directed our two *National Treasure* hits—in the director's chair, and with the wonder of contemporary New York City as the backdrop, we've tried very hard with *The Sorcerer's Apprentice* to honor those past wizards—Goethe, Dukas, and, especially, Walt Disney—while at the same time finding a magic of our own to weave around the audience.

ABOVE: Nicolas Cage and Jerry Bruckheimer on set at the Bedford Armory in Brooklyn. OPPOSITE: Concept art of Mickey Mouse as the Sorcerer's Apprentice for *Fantasia*.

It's quite a mandate, and one that we all took very seriously. We're proud of the results, and hopefully this book will tell and show you something about the painstaking process, from the artists both in front of and behind the camera who created *The Sorcerer's Apprentice*. Above all, I think we've found something of a real-life response to a question posed in the film by Dave Stutler to Balthazar Blake when he asks if sorcery is science or magic. We might also ask if movies are science or magic.

And the answer to both questions is the same as the one we found to so many of the questions raised in *The Sorcerer's Apprentice*—a resounding yes.

Prologue

Do You Believe in Magic?

Since time is obviously a relative concept, let's begin the story in the only possible place for a movie about sorcery and magic to begin—at the end—and then work backward to the beginning.

The date is Friday, July 10, 2009, and the setting is the cavernous interior of a 108-year-old monumental pile of brick and stone in the Crown Heights section of Brooklyn, New York, known as the Bedford Armory. The eighty-eighth day of principal photography of the Walt Disney Pictures/Jerry Bruckheimer Films production of *The Sorcerer's Apprentice* is about to come to an end, and so is the whole epic endeavor that has enveloped a cast and crew of considerable heft for several months.

The company has been asked to assemble in late afternoon, after it's been decided by director Jon Turteltaub that the shot just completed of Nicolas Cage standing on a huge audio-animatronic version of the Chrysler Building eagle gargoyle was, in fact, his final one for the film. Turteltaub, producer Jerry Bruckheimer, and various weather-beaten but undaunted members of the film crew crowd together to hear the director say, "Everyone here would agree that all of our lives as crew people would be easier and better if every movie star was like Nic Cage."

Applause from all, and then the usually reserved actor addresses his colleagues: "Actors always get applauded, but you guys make the movie. You work so hard, you're here from the first minute of the day to that last minute of the day. It's your focus, your concentration, your grace under pressure that made this movie. And to me, you're all magicians. You make something out of nothing, something good . . . not just good because you're all professionals, but good because it's on the right side of the line.

"This is a crazy time for trying to keep our kids smiling," Cage continues. "People are losing their jobs, people are frustrated, feelings are tense. But what you did, I think, will give children all over the world a chance to smile, and believe in magic and enchantment.

"If I could be so bold to say that maybe the greatest Merlinean of them all— perhaps he was Merlin himself, who knows?—Mr. Walt Disney, would be so proud of what you've done. Jon Turteltaub, you are going to continue on your path to make excellent movies that make families happy. And to the maestro, Jerry Bruckheimer, don't ever change. You keep people smiling, and families going to the movies. We're wrapping on day eighty-eight of production. Eight is, for those of us who know, a magical number. It's the number of the magician, and also the number of infinity.

"And to those of you who don't believe in magic," concluded Nicolas Cage, "today, our wrap day, is Nikola Tesla's birthday. And none of us knew it. So, there you go. Cheers."

And with that surprisingly emotional farewell, Cage is gone. As for Nikola Tesla? No, he isn't one of the grips on the movie. Tesla is the late, great genius of electrical engineering whose transcendent inventions and theorem changed the world. A man who proved time and again that just because something is not visible to the naked eye, that doesn't mean it doesn't exist.

So was wrapping on Tesla's 153rd birthday coincidence or magic?

The answer is yes.

Now flash back to four months earlier, on March 2, and an elegant, wood-paneled meeting room on the lower level of the Ritz-Carlton Hotel on Central Park South (that very day, presaging the miserable weather that would assail the company all the way through filming, the biggest snowstorm of the year hit New York). A group that includes producer Jerry Bruckheimer, director Jon Turteltaub, executive producers Mike Stenson, Chad Oman, Barry Waldman, Norm Golightly, and Todd Garner, screenwriters Doug Miro and Carlo Bernard, and the cast of the film sits around a long, rectangular table. It's the read-through of the script one week before the start of principal photography. "Let's go to work," says Jerry Bruckheimer, followed by a typically Turteltaub-ian quip, "and please hold all compliments until the end."

The chemistry and ease between the actors is remarkable, considering the fact that they all have just introduced themselves to each other. Nicolas Cage and Jay Baruchel already seem to have alchemically developed a repartee and ease in delivering dialogue on the printed page, as well as occasional improvisations. There's much laughter, quite a bit from Baruchel as he listens to Cage and Alfred Molina's dialogue exchanges.

Thus, two hundred twelve years after Johann Wolfgang von Goethe wrote his poem "Der Zauberlehrling," 112 years after Paul Dukas composed his orchestral "L'apprenti sorcier," based on that poem, and sixty-nine years after Walt Disney released his magnum opus, *Fantasia*, which included a famous episode based upon those older sources starring a character named Mickey Mouse, "The Sorcerer's Apprentice" was about to live again.

OPPOSITE: **Nicolas Cage on the mechanical version of the Chrysler eagle against a green screen, filmed at the Bedford Armory.**

SORCERERS

The Long Journey of
The Sorcerer's Apprentice

LEFT TO RIGHT: A unique lineage connects Johann Wolfgang von Goethe,
Paul Dukas, Walt Disney, and Jerry Bruckheimer.

When all is said and done—and there's been a lot said and done about *The Sorcerer's Apprentice* over the past 212 years—it's *fairly* safe to say that this will be the only time in history that Jerry Bruckheimer will produce a film based on a poem written by Johann Wolfgang von Goethe.

Then again, never say never.

If the great German author, thinker, and natural scientist himself could have peered into a crystal ball, could he have possibly imagined that his work of poetry ("Der Zauberlehrling" in the original language) would, in time, receive a big-scale, live-action treatment from Walt Disney Pictures, under the baton of megaproducer Jerry Bruckheimer and blockbuster director Jon Turteltaub? Doubtful.

The magic unleashed by Goethe has since pirouetted through the centuries, inspiring generations of readers, music lovers, and moviegoers to adapt and embrace it in their own way. And now it's this generation's turn to rediscover the timeless tale of sorcery as reimagined for the twenty-first century, with what Disney himself once referred to as "some old-fashioned magic called imagination."

Goethe's "Der Zauberlehrling": Hexenmeisters, Floods, and Broomsticks

Although Goethe (1749–1832) wrote his fourteen-stanza poem in 1797, thematic antecedents can be found far earlier in Lucian's short frame story *Philopseudes*, written in 150 AD. This story features a similar tale that must have influenced the great German writer (particularly considering Goethe's passion for ancient and world literature). But Goethe brought to "Der Zauberlehrling" something crucial that was lacking in *Philopseudes*: a clear moral. Goethe's poem is narrated by the apprentice himself, who upon being left to his own devices by his old "Hexenmeister" takes it upon himself to arrogantly demonstrate his own magical arts. The apprentice orders an old broomstick to wrap itself in rags, grow a head and two arms, and, with a bucket, prepare a bath for him.

The problem is, the living broomstick fills up not only the tub, but also every bowl and cup in the room. As one might suspect, the overly confident apprentice has forgotten the magic word to make it stop, resulting in a massive flood. The apprentice thinks he has a solution by taking an axe to the poor old broom, splitting it in twain. The result? Not one, but *two* living broomsticks. Finally the apprentice is bailed out, quite literally, by the return of the old hexenmeister, who quickly sends the broom back into the closet from whence it came, with an imprecation that it will return only when he, the true master, calls it forth once again to do his bidding.

It is a deceptively simple message, but timeless and profound. "What's great about the story is this little lesson about cutting corners, doing things the easy way, trying to fulfill this desire we all have to grow up a little too fast," notes Jon Turteltaub, the film's director. The lesson learned? Taking your time and learning before you leap is not a bad thing.

Dukas' "L'apprenti sorcier": A Poem's Sound Track

Exactly a century after Goethe wrote his famous poem, French composer and music teacher Paul Abraham Dukas (1865–1935) wrote his vastly popular ten-and-a-half-minute orchestral work, titled "L'apprenti sorcier." An immediate success for its brilliant musical coloration and rhythmic excellence, and its wonderfully jaunty "march of the broomsticks," the scherzo has truly stood the test of time. It is, to a popular audience anyway, Dukas' most enduring work. While perhaps less well known as others of his generation, Dukas was not only a highly respected composer in his time—studying at the Paris Conservatory under Theodore Dubois and Ernest Guiraud, befriending Claude Debussy in the process—but he also became a beloved teacher of composition to the next generation of musical artists, among them Olivier Messiaen, Carlos Chavez, and Manuel Ponce. He retains a place of honor in his resting place at Pere Lachaise Cemetery in Paris, along with so many other greats.

Fantasia: The Passion of Walt Disney

The combination of the story first told by Goethe and which later found superb musical expression in Dukas' composition must have had powerful appeal to Walt Disney. In the summer of 1937, while dining alone at Chasen's restaurant in Beverly Hills, the still youthful king of movie animation invited the famed conductor Leopold Stokowski to join him, and something extraordinary was conjured up between them.

At this time, Walt Disney had already utilized music as a foundation of his animated film series, *Silly Symphonies*. As the story goes, he discussed with Stokowski his desire for them to collaborate on a cartoon short based on Dukas' "The Sorcerer's Apprentice." The two men moved quickly, as great men often do. Disney secured the rights to the music, set his team of animators and writers to the task of developing the details of the short, and Stokowski recorded the scherzo on January 9, 1938. But that wasn't the end. Disney and Stokowski then agreed that "The Sorcerer's Apprentice" would be only one episode in a feature-length film that set more classical music to animated segments, initially known as *The Concert Feature* and later retitled *Fantasia*. It was to be the riskiest, most ambitious and innovative project of Walt Disney's career to that point and, it can be argued, of his entire life.

Fantasia was intentionally conceived to be a bridge between high and popular art. It would, they hoped, be a way to introduce on a mass scale serious classical and modern music to an audience who had little exposure to that kind of art, which today many take for granted. Spending months hermetically sealed inside his office at the new Walt Disney Studios in Burbank, California, Disney, Stokowski, and music critic Deems Taylor (who consulted on the film and later served as its narrator) listened to an endless number of recordings before deciding upon Bach's "Toccata and Fugue in D Minor," Pierne's "Cydalise and the Goat-Foot" (later replaced by a section of Beethoven's Sixth Symphony, the "Pastorale"), Tchaikovsky's "The Nutcracker Suite," Mussorgsky's "Night on Bald Mountain," Schubert's "Ave Maria," Ponchielli's "Dance of the Hours," Debussy's "Clair de Lune" (which was animated but later eliminated from the release version due to length), Stravinsky's

Walt Disney with conductor Leopold Stokowski.

"The Rite of Spring," and Dukas' "The Sorcerer's Apprentice."

The 125-minute *Fantasia*—unusually long even today for an animated feature film—opened to great fanfare on November 13, 1940, at the Broadway Theater in New York City. The music was enhanced by a multichannel sound system, called Fantasound, especially developed for the film, and was the first commercial motion picture ever to be exhibited with stereophonic sound. "The Sorcerer's Apprentice" episode, directed by James Algar (who went on to direct most of Disney's great nature films in the 1950s), cast the studio's biggest star, Mickey Mouse, in the title role, and thereby reinvented and reinvigorated the beloved character, who received a design makeover for the film.

Since then, *Fantasia* has meant something different to each successive generation. Ironically, the film didn't actually make a profit until its rerelease in 1969, when it caught on in a major way with the youth of the day as a massive "head trip." Soon

15

1940 poster for Walt Disney's *Fantasia*.

its redesigned psychedelic poster targeting teens and college students could be seen across the nation.

But the film has transcended trendiness, now standing as an eternal testament to Walt Disney's artistic ambitions and unshakable will to advance the art form of both animation and motion pictures by creating something that audiences had never before seen or heard. *Fantasia* is one of the films selected for preservation in the United States National Film Registry by the Library of Congress, and "The Sorcerer's Apprentice" episode is generally considered the best and most beloved episode of all. "Sorcerer Mickey" is one of the character's most popular incarnations, his blue conical hat emblazoned as an official symbol of Disney's Hollywood Studios at Walt Disney World and, in a huge version, seen at the entrance of the

Disney Animation Building in Burbank. "Sorcerer Mickey" is also the star of the smash nighttime spectacular Fantasmic! at Disney Theme Parks, defeating evil nightly to massive crowds.

A New Beginning

The cinematic rebirth of *The Sorcerer's Apprentice* originated with a passionate admirer of the Disney version . . . Nicolas Cage. "The idea came to me and my friend Todd Garner," he recalls. "I was making another movie at the time, and I wanted to explore a more magical and fantastic realm, where I could play a character who had mystical abilities. I shared these thoughts with Todd, and the next day we hit on the perfect project: *The Sorcerer's Apprentice*. We started getting different writers together over at my company, Saturn Films, with my producing partner Norm Golightly, and developing a story line that might be appealing to a studio. We went to Disney, and they loved the idea.

"We went forward with that for a few months," continues Cage, "and then it occurred to me that Jerry Bruckheimer would be the perfect producer to really put the project on a fast track with the Studio. He immediately sparked to it, and his ideas were just music to my ears."

"I've always liked stories that have a magical element, and 'The Sorcerer's Apprentice' is one of the great magical stories of all time," says Jerry Bruckheimer. "We thought it would be tremendously exciting to develop the core of that concept into a brand-new story set in the modern world."

The Sorcerer's Apprentice was right up Jerry Bruckheimer Films alley, notes executive producer Mike Stenson, the company's longtime president. "It's that combination of an interesting character story mixed with a lot of humor, and also a great fantasy element. So if you're talking about the kind of movie that will get everybody into the theater, you end up with a movie that kids can go see, that teenagers can think is cool, and that parents can also love. It's the kind of project that we're always looking for."

Becoming a part of *The Sorcerer's Apprentice* package almost as early as Bruckheimer and Cage was director Jon Turteltaub—in part because of the film itself. But one cannot overlook the more magical elements at play. In what can only be described as harmonic convergence, Turteltaub not only had an intense passion for the project and a love of *Fantasia* itself, but also a relationship with Cage and Bruckheimer that went back decades. It was, one might say, written in the stars. "Nic and I went to Beverly Hills High School together, and we were back there twenty-seven years later watching his son doing a play on the same stage where Nic and I had performed all those years ago," the filmmaker recalls. "Afterward, we were standing around talking, and Nic said, 'You know, I've got this movie that

I really want to do and wonder if you would be interested in it. We're going to do a retelling of "The Sorcerer's Apprentice."' It just sounded great. Done deal!"

"Jon was absolutely the perfect choice to bring the movie to life," says Jerry Bruckheimer. "Based not only upon the long professional relationship and friendship that he has with both Nic and myself, but also the sense of wonder and joy that he has both personally and artistically." Adds executive producer Chad Oman, president of production for Jerry Bruckheimer Films, "Jon is a kid at heart . . . a big kid, yes, but nevertheless, he still has the fascination and imagination of a kid. He was the right director for the project because he brings a wonderful sense of humor and an acute ability to bring out great characterization on-screen."

All of the major players behind *The Sorcerer's Apprentice* were tremendous admirers of Walt Disney's *Fantasia*. "To me," says Nicolas Cage, "it's the most beautiful movie ever made. I think *Fantasia* might have been the first movie my parents ever took me to see. It was my introduction to the movies, to Walt Disney animation, and also, naturally, to classical music. The imagery throughout the entire film just transported me, and even at that young age, I think it influenced my life. Everything affected me as a result of Walt Disney. I still watch *Fantasia* annually, lower the lights, and lose myself in the movie."

"*The Sorcerer's Apprentice* has such a great Disney pedigree to it," notes Turteltaub, "and I knew right away that I'd be dealing with something that had to be excellent, had to be special, had to live up to its important role within Disney and the history of film. That piece from *Fantasia* is as iconic as any eight minutes of film that has ever been created, so to be part of that was really exciting. You think, all right, where do you go with that?"

Where they ended up was with a story that, while full of both fantasy and magic, is at its core, a love story. After a rather mortifying event at the age of ten that results in Dave Stutler never professing his love for the young Becky Barnes— and meeting the mysterious Balthazar Blake—we flash forward ten years. Dave, now a college student simply trying to pass physics, still wishes to set things right with the girl of his dreams. But in movies nothing is simple, and Dave's world is turned upside down when the eccentric Balthazar suddenly reenters his life.

Balthazar himself is also tormented. He is a sorcerer embroiled in a centuries-long battle that pits the followers of two powerful sorcerers—the good Merlin and the evil Morgana—against each other for either the destruction or salvation of the world. Things reach a critical point when archnemesis and longtime Morganian rival Maxim Horvath is freed and threatens to release his fellow Morganians—Sun Lok, Abigail Williams, and Morgana herself—from the Grimhold. The Grimhold, an object that resembles a simple nesting doll, is actually a prison for these cruel and evil sorcerers. No simple toy indeed. Soon, a hapless Dave becomes Balthazar's

The sorcerer from "The Sorcerer's Apprentice" in *Fantasia* (1940).

reluctant protégé and finds himself facing off against a great evil—after only a brief crash course in the art and science of sorcery. Together, these unlikely partners must stop Horvath, the illusionist/Morganian Drake Stone (who is more fond of being famous than being a villain), and the rest of the Morganian forces from destroying humanity itself. They must also find a way to save both their loves from cruel—and perhaps deadly—fates.

"It's a story about two quests," explains Jerry Bruckheimer. "Balthazar has been searching the world through the centuries for his apprentice, and Dave then has to discover his true potential as a human being. Dave is a very serious student and doesn't need or want Balthazar in his life, or to be a sorcerer. But Balthazar is like a fly that keeps buzzing around, tormenting this poor kid until he succumbs to becoming this magical character, which I think every kid would want to be. But if someone showed up at your door and said that you're really a sorcerer, you wouldn't believe them, either.

"But in the course of the story," Bruckheimer continues, "you see the relationship build between the two of them, and how Balthazar gives Dave the confidence that he needs, not only with his sorcery, but also his personal life."

"What the story is really about is your imagination," adds Jon Turteltaub, "and thinking about what would happen if sorcery was real and present and in New York

City today. And imagine if someone came to you and said that you're going to be a great sorcerer. It would kind of upset your life a little bit; you'd have to call your orthodontist and say, 'I need to make the appointment at four o'clock, not two o'clock.' How do you get an average everyday person who's been struggling a lot with his own image and success, someone less than ordinary, and turn him into somebody extraordinary?"

Following an initial draft of the script by the respected writing team of Larry Konner and Mark Rosenthal (*The Jewel of the Nile*, Disney's *Mighty Joe Young*, *Mona Lisa Smile*)—which established some of the characters and locations of the story—a vibrantly talented young screenwriter named Matt Lopez entered the project. Lopez, who originally emerged from the Studio's writer's program and had written/cowritten Disney's *Bedtime Stories* and *Race to Witch Mountain*, was approached for his own take on the story.

"*The Sorcerer's Apprentice* was such a passion project for Nic," says Lopez. "In our first meeting he came in with a huge stack of books about sorcery, which was very inspiring to me. The challenge was, how do you reinterpret magic and show it on-screen in a way that people haven't seen before? I made the character of Dave Stutler grounded in science and dedicated to the pursuit of physics, which I thought was an exciting direction to take for a couple of reasons. One, you have a character devoted to the rational world and explaining everything in objective, scientific terms. That's Dave. And you put him together with Balthazar, the sorcerer, who sees everything in magical terms. What I think excited people about my take was that you find out these two worlds are actually one, that sorcery is to physics what alchemy is to chemistry. There's a key line in which Balthazar tells Dave that everything they do as sorcerers is within the laws of physics . . . that he just doesn't know all of the laws yet. That is the core creative idea behind sorcery in the movie. I love science, and I think grounding it in that way is unexpected, and will be really exciting on-screen."

Adds Turteltaub, "In the film, science and magic are inextricably linked, you cannot have one without the other. If you look at magic as your imagination and science as fact, the two is where invention and creation come from. You have to have imagination, and you have to have truth."

"We tried to keep everything in the realm of science," adds Lopez. "In the original version of the script, the sorcerers used the traditional wands. And in our first meeting, we said that wands are cool, but they've been used again and again. We wanted there to be something else that helped them actually conduct this sorcery. In my first meeting with Nic, I noticed that he had this incredible ring with a green stone, and I asked him about it. He told me some of the history of the ring, which he bought in a shop in New Orleans. I started thinking that rings should be the conductor of this sorcery, converting one form of energy or matter into another, which is what Dave is experimenting with in physics. What he comes to realize is that by doing this science he is subconsciously also doing the sorcery, which scared him so much when he encountered Balthazar and Horvath at such a young age."

Lopez notes that in Goethe's original poem, and even in the *Fantasia* episode, "it all ends very abruptly with the apprentice once again relegated to essentially the sorcerer's janitor. You never get to see the apprentice grow into the role of becoming a sorcerer himself, which we thought would be fun to see. We also don't get to see the sorcerer teaching the apprentice magic, so we have Balthazar do that with Dave. Except that because of the circumstances, something that should take ten years to learn must be taught in a few days."

Matt Lopez also introduced elements of the Matter of Britain—the mythology of the Arthurian tradition—into the story, which seemed a natural fit. "We had produced *King Arthur*, which to some degree intentionally sought to demystify Arthurian mythology and root it more in believable history," notes Jerry Bruckheimer. "So it was time for us to restore the stories to the realm of legend and magic."

Adds executive producer Chad Oman, "The Arthurian element gave us a myth to play with, and a really great backstory. We loved the idea of starting it all with Merlin, and so did Nic."

"As a child I was very interested in Arthurian legend," says Lopez, "so I brought into the script two camps of rival sorcery, the antagonistic followers of Merlin and Morgana. There are certain medieval accounts which state that Morgana was once Merlin's apprentice, so I thought that a schism between them would create two rival camps that have been in competition for centuries. I thought, what if this is still going on, even in modern-day New York City, but known only to a select few."

In the magic-or-coincidence category, Matt Lopez enthusiastically notes, "I largely wrote the script for *The Sorcerer's Apprentice* on the third floor of the old Animation Building at Walt Disney Studios in Burbank, the same building that Walt built in 1938 when they moved from Hollywood. My office is literally where 'The Sorcerer's Apprentice' sequence in *Fantasia* was animated, and that's something I took a lot of pride in. It's an unbroken chain of Disney history that we've come full circle all these years later."

> There's a key line in which Balthazar tells Dave that everything they do as sorcerers is within the laws of physics . . . that he just doesn't know all of the laws yet. —MATT LOPEZ

For a flashback scene, Dean Tschetter illustrates a medieval battle.

their boundaries? Based on that, I came up with the Merlin Circle and other guidelines of sorcery. Jerry also gave me one of the best pieces of writing advice I've ever gotten, which was that I had made Dave such a shut-in and sad sack, that it would be hard for the audience to root for a character who's not rooting for himself. Jerry thought that Dave should be a nerd, but a *cool* nerd."

Notes Jon Turteltaub, "Balthazar and Dave both wish the other wasn't in their lives. Balthazar needs an apprentice, but he certainly doesn't need Dave. Dave, for his part, doesn't want to have anything to do with this crazy person who intrudes on his life. So they annoy each other. But they're both bright, and able to see the right way to tease and bother the other person, and try to get them to either shape up or leave them alone.

"Dave, who's an intellectual physics student, just wants to know the real, factual truth about everything. He needs to open up and see that there's a whole world that he didn't previously think could possibly exist; and then continue to take that and realize all the possibilities in himself that hadn't existed before," Turteltaub concludes. "That's a huge part of Dave's journey."

Enter Miro and Bernard

"Matt Lopez worked with us on the screenplay of the movie for a year," says Chad Oman. "He probably wrote about seven drafts during that time period, and his contributions were enormously helpful. [Screenwriters] Carlo Bernard and Doug Miro joined the team about six weeks prior to shooting. We had just finished a solid year of working with them during prep and production on *Prince of Persia: The Sands of Time*, so we knew they worked well under pressure and that they could bring a fresh perspective to the story. In a very short amount of time, Doug and Carlo introduced a substantial number of new ideas to the movie. And just as on *Prince of Persia*, both Doug and Carlo stayed involved throughout shooting."

"It was unique by coming on later in the process," notes Carlo Bernard, "but we were able to be inspired by the casting that had already been done, as well as by the things that Jon Turteltaub was sending us in terms of location and production design, which showed us visually what an exciting world was being created in New York. They stuck us in a room, and Jerry and Jon had them cover the walls with pictures of the production design and locations, and we pretty much stayed there seven days a week. Steve Yamamoto's fantastic previsualizations were also really helpful."

"The writers who preceded us brought a lot of great invention to the script, and we were also inspired by what they wrote," adds Doug Miro. "Our hope was to take the strengths of the existing script and just try to have even more fun with it in terms of characters," says Bernard.

With such passion and dedication fueling the film, the urgency to get it on-screen increased tremendously. The film was "fast-tracked." Work started immediately—and it was intense. "Jerry read my first draft of the script and really liked it, but felt that there needed to be a clearer understanding on the part of the audience of the rules of magic," recalls Matt Lopez. "I thought this was a great insight on Jerry's part, because audiences do want to know what's possible. Can sorcerers fly? Are they immortal? What can they do? What can't they do? What are

Craig Mullins's illustration of the sorcerer-training sequence, with Dave Stutler fielding plasma bolts from Balthazar Blake.

The writing team immediately caught the beam of the story's essence. "It's a classic hero story," says Bernard. "Dave's journey is ultimately of someone who doesn't believe in himself and doesn't think he's capable of accomplishing something great, and realizing over the course of the story that, to his great surprise, he actually is capable of being a hero. His relationship with both Balthazar and Becky serves to take him on that journey. For us, in the structure of that story was our guiding light.

"I think that translates in a concrete way, perhaps, to recognizing your true talents," Bernard goes on. "Dave is a talented guy, but he doesn't seem to give himself credit for it. When Balthazar and Becky both point out his talents, it helps Dave to see who he really is, and gain strength from that. I also think that Balthazar embodies the idea of putting mankind above yourself, the idea that there are greater things out there that mean more than any individual. That's a great concept, a warrior who has fought for man for a thousand years.

"Another theme of the movie," Bernard concludes, "which comes directly from the original story, is that you have to earn the magic, that you can't cast a spell that you are not capable of controlling."

Almost immediately following the blood, sweat, and tears they devoted to many months of labor on *Prince of Persia: The Sands of Time*, on which they either alternatively or collectively spent time on set in sweltering Morocco and the admittedly more temperate London, Doug Miro and Carlo Bernard were more than happy to continue their association with Jerry Bruckheimer. "Jerry gets movies made, which I think is a feat of magic in itself, but he always has the audiences' well-being in mind," observes Bernard. "Jerry's great at coming in and being our reality check, and providing a very commonsense approach. He can project what's on the page to the way an audience is going to experience it sitting in a theater, which is a tremendously important insight."

"Jerry is incredibly supportive, particularly of writers," adds Miro. "He is so aware of the fact that we have an audience locked in a theater for two hours, and their time is in our hands, so we've got to make the best possible use of it. It's not a book they can put down, it's not an iPod on which they can skip a track."

Miro and Bernard also delighted in working with Jon Turteltaub. "I was especially impressed by Jon's handle on tone and character," says Bernard. "Jon was really great at bringing everything back to character, trying to keep it real and grounding it in the human experience. A situation can't lapse into something that feels like a movie situation. Jon gives you realistic-feeling characters in real situations, has a great BS detector for stuff that feels contrived, strained, or familiar. Jon had a kind of mantra for us and everybody involved, which was to always keep things surprising. Jerry's also a stickler for logic, which was important to Jon, too. We couldn't give the characters a blank check, there had to be rules."

As always, as the script was developed and crafted, there were changes, some of them major. One of these was the ultimate exclusion from the final draft of Chernabog, the demonic, terrifying creature from yet another episode of *Fantasia*, "Night on Bald Mountain."

"Chernabog was such an iconic *Fantasia* character, and we were sort of just sticking him in the movie," Jon Turteltaub explains. "Then we all felt, wait, this guy's too great and important, so let's pray the movie does well so we get a chance to make another one and give Chernabog a better part.

"But you should meet Chernabog's agent. You think wolves get mad when you don't use them?" Turteltaub quips, referring to the animal actors who were to appear in *The Sorcerer's Apprentice*. "Well, Chernabog's just awful!"

Illustrator Tani Kunitake envisioned Chernabog for the film, although ultimately the demonic character from *Fantasia* is not seen in the final version.

MAGICIANS

CLOCKWISE FROM TOP LEFT: Nicolas Cage's hair and makeup artist, Ilona Herman, makes some adjustments to his hair before the cameras roll; Jay Baruchel and Gregory Woo prepare to work on a chilly night on Eldridge Street in New York's Chinatown; Balthazar Blake in the colorful acupuncturist's shop in Chinatown; confetti and lanterns enliven the set dressing on Eldridge Street.

Jerry Bruckheimer
Master Illusionist

If Jerry Bruckheimer can be described as a magician, then he's a man who's been pulling rabbits out of hats for nearly forty years as one of Hollywood's most truly legendary producers.

Making a movie is like being one of those marvelous Chinese acrobats who manage to keep three dozen plates spinning at the same time, requiring the most exquisite sense of balance and timing. One wrong move, and all the plates go plummeting down, resulting in a billion shattered and useless shards. Bruckheimer has made very few such moves in his four decades of providing worldwide audiences with film and television entertainment. Not only have his films been massively, record-shatteringly successful, but time and again they have influenced popular culture, from fashion trends like one-shouldered sweatshirts (*Flashdance*) and flight jackets (*Top Gun*), to changing the creative face of television with the *CSI* programs, to the glorious resurrection of an entire moribund genre with the *Pirates of the Caribbean* trilogy.

"The way you do anything is the way you do everything," says the anonymous, Zen-like adage that hangs in the photocopy room of Jerry Bruckheimer's impressive but unpretentious headquarters on a nondescript industrial street in Santa Monica, California. In other words, everything should be approached with the same striving toward excellence, whether the task is small or large. And it is that attention to detail that is one of the keys to Jerry Bruckheimer's stupendous, Alger-esque success story.

The son of modest German-immigrant parents, he grew up in Detroit, graduated from the University of Arizona, and then entered the advertising and TV commercial business in Chicago. A film and photography buff from early childhood, Bruckheimer further discovered the power of the image to tell a story while working in advertising. Making the move into producing in the early 1970s, Bruckheimer explored ways to take full advantage of film (and then television) as a pure, visual medium, while at the same time hiring some of the best writers in Hollywood to match word with image.

While there may not be a "the buck stops here" sign on his desk, ultimately,

Bruckheimer embraces the full responsibilities of his position as producer and chief of Jerry Bruckheimer Films and Television (as well as the brand-new Jerry Bruckheimer Games division) with great attention to every detail. But at the same time, he has the wisdom to allow those he enlists, both on staff and as creative and production personnel on his films and television programs, to do their jobs.

Jerry Bruckheimer is, very simply, one of the most successful film and television producers in entertainment history. Eighteen films from the producer, whose famous lightning bolt logo can be seen at the beginning of each title, have earned domestic U.S. box office revenues of over $100 million. And many have been acknowledged with numerous honors, including forty-one Academy Award nominations, six Oscars, eight Grammy Award nominations, five Grammys, twenty-three Golden Globe nominations, four Golden Globes, eighty-eight Emmy Award nominations, and eighteen Emmys.

Emerging from the world of advertising, Bruckheimer's producing career began with such films as *Farewell, My Lovely* and *American Gigolo*. With producing partner Don Simpson, the pair made one hit after another, including *Top Gun*, *Days of Thunder*, *Beverly Hills Cop* and *Beverly Hills Cop II*, *Bad Boys*, *Dangerous Minds*, *Crimson Tide*, and *The Rock*. Following Simpson's passing in 1996, Bruckheimer went on to produce even greater hits, among them *Con Air*, *Armageddon*, *Enemy of the State*, *Gone in 60 Seconds*, *Remember the Titans*, *Pearl Harbor*, *Black Hawk Down*, *Glory Road*, *National Treasure* and its follow-up *National Treasure: Book of Secrets*, *Déjà Vu*, *Confessions of a Shopaholic*, *G-Force*, *Prince of Persia: The Sands of Time*, and, let us not forget, the landmark *Pirates of the Caribbean* trilogy.

But movies are not his only passion. In 1997 he created Jerry Bruckheimer Television, which has become a powerhouse of the medium. Some of the company's hugely popular programs have included the landmark *CSI* and its spin-offs, *CSI: Miami* and *CSI: NY*, *Cold Case*, *Without a Trace*, and seven-time Emmy Award–winning *The Amazing Race*.

The secret to his success? When asked, which happens often, Bruckheimer always responds, simply and directly, "I make movies and TV shows that I want to see. I'm not sure what other people like, but I know what *I* like." Luckily, what Jerry Bruckheimer likes seems to be what the rest of the world likes as well, and part of the reason is that he's never separated himself from the mass audience to which he's always appealed. "If something doesn't make sense to Jerry, it's probably a good guess that it's not going to make sense to an audience," says executive producer Mike Stenson, president of Jerry Bruckheimer Films. "He has an absolute sixth sense about what works in a movie, and what doesn't."

"Jerry is the biggest advocate of artists and artistic creativity that I've ever worked with," says Jon Turteltaub. "He loves bringing in talented people. He doesn't chase box-office stars, he chases talent and wants you to bring out the best in these people. He also pushes more than any person I've ever worked with, and he's the guy you desperately don't want to disappoint. He's never unfriendly, he's never not nice, never not polite . . . you just want him happy. I think it's because we all know that he knows 'good' when he sees it, and if Jerry doesn't like it he's probably right. He has a better sense of the audience than anyone I've ever spoken to. He knows what people want to see when they're going to the movies. They're not the judging panel for the Oscars, they're people going to the movies, so Jerry wants to give them a great night out."

"Jerry's presence on set always makes things better," says Academy Award–winning special-effects coordinator John Frazier, who has previously worked on many of the producer's biggest films, including *Armageddon* and *Pearl Harbor*. "I don't know what it is, but Jerry is this magical guy. When he's on set, you know that everything is going to work out fine. He knows how to pick a team that can work well together. Jerry's just so talented at what he does, and he cares so much about the quality of his films."

Actors certainly seem to love working on Jerry Bruckheimer's films, considering the vast number of them who have returned to the fold more than once. On *The Sorcerer's Apprentice* alone, Nicolas Cage, Alfred Molina, and Toby Kebbell are all returnees from other Bruckheimer films. Nicolas Cage, who has now enjoyed seven collaborations with the producer, noted that "working with Jerry, it's miraculous how it all happens. He creates a spontaneous environment in which you can't help but search into the deepest part of your creative energy to find a solution to every issue. It's like jazz. Everyone starts coming up with ideas at the spur of the moment that are very fresh and electric. On Jerry's movies, you're on a high wire without a net, and every time something good comes out of it. That's what keeps me coming back, and I'd like to think that's what keeps Jerry coming back to me."

Regarding the joys of working on a Jerry Bruckheimer production, Alfred Molina notes that "in Jerry's movies, there's a wonderful combination of action, adventure, comedy, and great characters, and the films are full of depth and detail. They really take you someplace different, there's nothing pedestrian or everyday about them."

"I grew up watching every Jerry Bruckheimer movie," confesses Jay Baruchel, who had previously been cast by the producer as the star of the television series *Just Legal*. "I remember my friends and I buying tickets for another movie and then sneaking into *Con Air* when we were fifteen years old. It's a pretty mind-blowing experience to see the worlds that Jerry creates."

Says Toby Kebbell, who most recently costarred alongside Jake Gyllenhaal in *Prince of Persia: The Sands of Time*, "What's fun about doing Jerry's films is that he creates the perfect environment for you to do the stuff you dreamt of doing when you were a kid, like swing a sword or have energy come out of your hands. And the man loves film. When Jerry comes to set, he always looks excited and enthusiastic about the whole enterprise. It's not just about him being an important person, but a real participant."

"I respect Jerry Bruckheimer very much because he's had a huge impact in Hollywood and all over the world," says Italian-born, Paris-based international star Monica Bellucci. "For me, as a European, it's great to be part of his project."

Notes executive producer Chad Oman, president of production of Jerry Bruckheimer Films, "The thing that's interesting about Jerry is that he always looks at the big picture. From the beginning of developing a story or a concept, he's already on multiple tracks: who's the audience, what will the poster look like, how do I sell this movie? Jerry also knows every aspect of filmmaking. He has the ability to come into the editing room and see a cut of the movie, and without taking notes he can sit there for three days afterward and give detailed verbal notes about scenes, shots, and structure. I've never seen anything like it before."

That's confirmed by William Goldenberg, film editor of *The Sorcerer's Apprentice* and five other Bruckheimer movies. "What's great to me is when a producer can come in and give you an overview of the movie. Jerry lets you do your job and he expects excellence, but at the same time he has great input. He does what great producers do. He looks at the big picture, but can give really fine detail too."

Jerry Bruckheimer long ago realized that films are, and have always been, a form of enchantment spun by dreamers . . . an enchantment that's never lost its appeal to him after four decades as Hollywood's master illusionist. "When the lights go down and the screen lights up, its magic time," he says. "What was true in the early silent era is no less true now. Cinema is the place where dreams and technology meet, but rather than collide, they merge into something truly special. I still can't think of a better way to spend two hours than at the movies. Pass the popcorn!"

CLOCKWISE FROM TOP LEFT: Jon Turteltaub's intensity is captured by Jerry Bruckheimer's camera; Nicolas Cage on the set of Drake Stone's penthouse balcony at the Bedford Armory; Isabella the bulldog (who actually portrays Tank, a male!) takes a well-deserved break on the training-room set; Balthazar Blake (Nicolas Cage) deep in thought in the underground training room.

Jon Turteltaub
The J. T. Touch

"One of the coolest, funniest, and most patient men on the planet," is how Dame Helen Mirren described her *National Treasure: Book of Secrets* director, Jon Turteltaub. And another one of the many wonderful things about Jon Turteltaub is that what you see in front of you is also what you get on-screen, a direct transmission of this filmmaker's personality: enthusiasm, incredibly quick wit, vibrant creativity, courage, relentless intelligence, and imagination, with more than a touch of warmth and humanity, qualities that made him the perfect choice to direct *The Sorcerer's Apprentice*. "A director's never bored," Turteltaub said at one point during the film's shoot, and it can safely be said that neither is anyone working on his sets.

"Jon is a consummate filmmaker, and we're very lucky to have worked with him twice in the past on very successful pictures," says Jerry Bruckheimer, speaking of their previous collaborations on the blockbuster duo of *National Treasure* and *National Treasure: Book of Secrets*. "Besides being a wonderful craftsman, Jon is a great storyteller. He also knows how to develop characters, and that's what you want from a director."

Confirms Nicolas Cage, who starred in the two *National Treasure* films, "It's always exciting to see an artist break out and go into another direction, reinvent himself, which is what I think Jon is doing with *The Sorcerer's Apprentice*. Jon is very good with comedy and knows how to get some humor out of a scene that I may not be looking for; and on the opposite side, he looks to me to go into the more enigmatic and mystical aspect of my character. He's done a really great job on this film."

It didn't hurt matters that, as mentioned, Cage and director Jon Turteltaub already had a friendship dating back to their days as classmates at high school in Los Angeles. "Socially, we were kind of on opposite ends of the tracks," Turteltaub recalled during the filming of *National Treasure: Book of Secrets*. "I was kind of the comfortable, funny kid who liked to be in musicals. Nic was a tough, smart,

Jon Turteltaub directs Alfred Molina and Nicolas Cage during a sorcerer's confrontation in the Arcana Cabana.

brooding, suspicious guy who had this air of rebel about him. We ended up teasing each other mercilessly in a really warm way."

"We were friendly, but there was always a little competitive tension there," confirmed Cage about his high school years with Turteltaub. "And working together on the *National Treasure* films, Jon and I became closer friends than we were in high school. By now there's a genuine bond."

Turteltaub's bond with Jerry Bruckheimer and Nicolas Cage also extends to Walt Disney Motion Pictures, having made all nine of his movies for the Studio: *3 Ninjas*, which was the Studio's most profitable film of 1992; the sleeper hit comedy *Cool Runnings*, which was Disney's highest-grossing live-action film of 1993; *While You Were Sleeping*, the breakout romantic comedy that helped to launch Sandra Bullock to stardom, in 1995; *Phenomenon*, one of the highest-grossing films of 1996, which starred John Travolta; the Touchstone Pictures thriller *Instinct*, starring Anthony Hopkins and Cuba Gooding Jr.; *The Kid*, a 2000 hit fantasy starring Bruce Willis; and, of course, the two *National Treasure* films, which collectively amassed a worldwide box-office tally of more than $800 million. That's quite a run, and clearly marked Jon Turteltaub as the perfect filmmaker to take on a project that has its roots in one of the Studio's most immortal films.

Among Turteltaub's newest, and perhaps now biggest, fans are the actors under his astute direction in *The Sorcerer's Apprentice*. "Jon is really an actor's director," states Alfred Molina, who himself is an actor's actor. "He's got a way of making absolutely clear what he means and what he expects, and how to find it. He's very even-tempered, not a martinet or diva in any way. Jon creates a nice mood. He's funny, likes to laugh, enjoys the camaraderie of the day. More than that, he's got a great eye for what works. He also loves movies, so he's coming from a point of not

28

just talent and intelligence, but also enthusiasm, which is really important."

"He's a fun dude, and knows how to make these movies," says Jay Baruchel. "I'm so honored that even on a movie of this size and stature, Jon still allows me to improvise and do my own thing. He's been incredibly giving in terms of letting me do what I want with the character. *Cool Runnings* and *3 Ninjas* were two of my favorite movies when I was a kid, so it was a real treat to work for Jon."

Adds Teresa Palmer, "Jon has this incredible energy, and urges us to do whatever feels natural and organic, rather than be locked into a particular way of playing. That's great, because I feel liberated and like I can try different things and not be embarrassed if it doesn't work."

Jon Turteltaub is not only a major feature film heavyweight, but a major force in television with his production company, Junction Entertainment. He made TV history producing and directing the highly acclaimed CBS drama *Jericho*. The prime-time show, which centered around a nuclear explosion that plunged the residents of a small, peaceful Kansas town into chaos, became a cult program and a cause célèbre when a fan campaign convinced the network to bring the show back for a second run after it was initially canceled. Turteltaub was also the executive producer of the innovative thirteen-part series *Harper's Island*, a thriller mystery for CBS in which the killer was revealed only in the final episode. The latter also won some passionate fans, including author Stephen King, who in the pages of *Entertainment Weekly* magazine, called it his favorite most recent network show.

As early as 1998, Turteltaub also made a substantial contribution to one of the most critically acclaimed and artistically important miniseries in history, *From the Earth to the Moon*, for which he directed the seventh of ten episodes. "That's All There Is" depicted the camaraderie of the crew of Apollo 12. For his efforts, Turteltaub was nominated by the Directors Guild of America for Outstanding Directorial Achievement in Movies for Television.

Show business flows through Turteltaub's blood. He was born in New York City and raised in Beverly Hills, the son of Saul Turteltaub, an iconic television producer whose credits included such classic programs as *Sanford & Son*, *What's Happening!!*, *That Girl*, and *Love, American Style*. The younger Turteltaub received his bachelor's degree at Wesleyan University in Connecticut and achieved his master's degree at the famed University of Southern California Film School.

Usually called "JT" by his crew members and colleagues, Jon Turteltaub brings a rare gift to contemporary filmmaking: a genuinely charming, unpretentious touch, in which he seamlessly weaves action and adventure with romance and humor, albeit laced with twenty-first-century sensibilities. Working with equal deftness in multiple genres, Turteltaub happily recalls classic Hollywood directors whose talents weren't limited to a narrow field. The first man on the set in the morning and

practically the last to leave, Turteltaub's working style combines incredibly hard work and encyclopedic knowledge of filmmaking. Cascades of brilliant and sometimes witheringly barbed one-liners and zingers have their sting softened by his genuine warmth and affection for those on the receiving end. Actually, the often humorously self-deprecating Turteltaub usually saves his sharpest stingers for himself. Thanking the crew at the end of the arduous shoot, Turteltaub said, "You're all just amazing. A lot of long nights, lots of rain, lots of bad tempers . . . alright, *one* bad temper. I know I did some yelling."

Jon Turteltaub is also the kind of man who gladly welcomes children from the Make-A-Wish Foundation to the set, and turns them into minidirectors, allowing them to call "action" and "cut" in "video village" (the area in which he and the other top creatives watch the monitors) and patiently explaining the filmmaker process. And in one instance, Turteltaub happened to meet some visitors to New York from the Midwest, who found themselves invited by him to the Chinatown set to watch night shooting of one of the biggest sequences in the movie. In other words, this guy is a classic mensch. And if you don't know what that means, it's time to book a trip to New York City.

As both a director and producer, Turteltaub has an appreciative overview of the entire filmmaking process. "Making a movie is like a building being able to sway a little bit in the wind," observes executive producer Barry Waldman, "because you never know when you come to work every day which way that wind is going to be blowing. This is my third movie with Jon, and he understands that part of the process. He's very approachable with changes and things that come up at the last minute, and how can we make it better with the time and situation that we have."

"The film is about turning what's around you into a magical space," says Jon Turteltaub of *The Sorcerer's Apprentice*. He turned that concept into a daily reality.

"I feel like we're all apprentices," said sound department boom operator T.R. Boyce toward the latter part of the shoot. "Every day is magic, and you never know what Jon is going to conjure up next."

A devoted family man, Turteltaub was often visited on set in New York by his effortlessly beautiful and elegant wife, Amy, and their endlessly lovable little boy, Jack (not to mention their huge, shaggy, gentle dog, a massive Leonberger named Archie, a set fixture who was often as much of an attraction to tourists as the film's stars). At one point, while the company was shooting at the historic Apthorp Apartments on the Upper West Side, then eighteen-month-old Jack Turteltaub was enjoying himself by purloining Maxim Horvath's ornate cane from Alfred Molina, and repeating "ho-cus po-cus." This coming from a boy who had only recently developed the capacity to put syllables together.

Now, *that's* real magic!

CONJURERS

Nicolas Cage
Balthazar Blake

THE X FACTOR

"We've been lucky enough to work with Nic seven times," says Jerry Bruckheimer of the actor who's starred in more of his productions than any other. "He's just a generous, brilliant actor, and fortunately, he likes the material that we develop, and we certainly liked *The Sorcerer's Apprentice*, which he brought to us."

The admiration between Cage and Bruckheimer is a two-way street, evident in the fact that they have worked over the years on everything from action blockbusters like *The Rock* to CGI creations like *G-Force*. It's clearly a match made in Hollywood heaven. "Jerry and I have a comfort level together," explains the actor. "He has his process, and Jerry understands my algebraic addition to that—the 'X factor,' if you will—that I think he's always looking for. There's a shorthand that we both get, I know how Jerry works, and vice versa."

"I'm going to make a bold statement," says director Jon Turteltaub. "I think that Balthazar Blake is the most perfect role that Nicolas Cage has ever had, and he's phenomenal in it. You never feel like Balthazar is a pushover, but you know that when he's on your side looking after you, you're in good hands."

It may come as an astonishing surprise, or perhaps not at all, that Nicolas Cage has now been a major-league, bona fide, A-list, big-opening-guaranteed movie star for almost thirty years. That's a veritable lifetime for any profession, but in the notoriously fickle world of show business, Cage's longevity at the top of his game represents the true measure of his astonishing range as an artist. Nicolas Cage is that rarity in the history of the medium, in equal measures a leading man and character actor . . . not alternately, but *simultaneously*.

Cage is an actor who has the ability to shift gears with more ease than a Formula 1 driver, marching to the beat of his own drummer, whether that means essaying an Academy Award–winning portrayal of a suicidal alcoholic in *Leaving Las Vegas*; giving brilliantly eccentric comedic performances in the likes of *Moonstruck* and *Raising Arizona*; getting his freak on in such beyond-the-edge films as David Lynch's *Wild at Heart* and Werner Herzog's more recent *Bad Lieutenant: Port of Call New Orleans*; finding the dramatic heart of *Lord of War* and Oliver Stone's *World Trade Center*; flexing his muscles in such action spectaculars as Jerry Bruckheimer's productions of *The Rock* and *Con Air* and John Woo's *Face/Off*; using brains more than brawn in Bruckheimer and Jon Turteltaub's two *National Treasure* films; or indulging his love of genre films, comics, and graphic novels on-screen in *Ghost Rider* and *Kick-Ass*. He acts because he loves it, chooses projects because he finds them intriguing, and eschews strategic master plans to his career "arc." And that's the way it's been from the beginning of his career.

And, like Turteltaub says, if ever there was a role in said career that Nicolas Cage was born to play, it's Balthazar Blake, student of Merlin, Sorcerer of the 777th Degree.

ABOVE: Michael Kaplan's designs of Balthazar's look, including his signature long leather coat and modified fedora, resembling a sorcerer's hat, in this costume development sketch by Brian Valenzuela.

"I think anyone who knows Nic knows that this is as polite and kind a person as you'll ever meet," says Turteltaub. "But there's also something inherently mysterious about Nic that he brings to the role of Balthazar, something unpredictable. Balthazar is edgy, dark, a little weird, a little unapproachable. But the more you get to know him—similarly to Nic—you realize a lot of that is just the fun stuff. There's a real soul right there.

"Balthazar is an ancient character who has seen it all, experienced it all, knows human nature really well, and has the wisdom, but also the fatigue, that comes from that," adds Turteltaub. "When you know the truth and you've looked behind the curtain, it sort of takes away a lot of your idealism toward life. He's a little bit cynical and tired of it, but also finds a lot of it very humorous. And Balthazar, at his essence, is a noble and really heroic character who has made extraordinary sacrifices for mankind without getting any credit. Nic brings all of that into his character. He is one of the most interesting people I've ever known, the most courageous, the most bold, the least ashamed.

"And you always get the thing that you yourself never could have thought of," finishes Turteltaub. "However many ideas you have—and believe me, every director knows in their mind exactly what everything is supposed to be, whether it's right or wrong, they have a version of it—Nic's version is never that. And as a result, you always get something surprising, special, different. He elevates the movie, makes it unique, and prevents it from ever being boring."

"Nic plays the slightly impatient, slightly irascible sorcerer to perfection," says executive producer Chad Oman. "He is great at being both intense and funny simultaneously. He played the part with the perfect mixture of edge and humor."

"He's just the Man," says Jay Baruchel unabashedly of Cage. "Forming a relationship with Nic has been the coolest thing for me by far. I've been a fan of his for pretty much my entire life, I've gone to see him in movies so many times. He has such a unique, distinct, iconic way of speaking, his cadences are unlike anyone else's. To hear that in conversations that we have together, and to act with him, is absolutely incredible.

"Beyond that," continues Baruchel, "I just enjoy his company. All the days we were shooting the car chase, where it's just me and Nic driving or getting towed through Midtown Manhattan, we had no choice but to keep each other company and make each other laugh. I've heard myriad anecdotes from his storied career, and it's been just amazing."

Added Alfred Molina toward the end of *The Sorcerer's Apprentice* shoot, "I've had a wonderful time with Nic. He's very generous, has great enthusiasm for the work he does, and enjoys other people's work. So when you come up with something that's maybe a bit different from what was indicated in the script, he's not one of those actors who says, 'Oh, that's not what we rehearsed.' He enjoys other people's creativity and contributions to the process. Nic also has a great sense of humor. Like a lot of wonderful actors, he understands that we take the work seriously, but you can't really take yourself too seriously while doing it."

Toby Kebbell, who, like Jay Baruchel, watched Nicolas Cage on-screen when he was still a kid,

TOP: **Artistic portrait of Nicolas Cage as Balthazar Blake by Gregory Hill.** LEFT: **Photographic portrait by Robert Zuckerman captures the character's essence.**

Part III

admits that "working with Nic, I was scared. I was worried that I wouldn't be good enough. But working with Nic was brilliant, because he makes you work really hard to create something great in order to just come somewhere close to his level of ability. That really helped me put my heart and soul into it. He's just a fascinating human being and genuinely one of our greatest actors."

On set, Nicolas Cage is quiet, thoughtful, determined, but unfailingly polite to fellow actors and crew. There is unquestionably a mystique and enigmatic air about him, none of it created for effect. "Nic doesn't try to make himself mysterious," noted one company member. "He actually *is* mysterious!" But he's not always aloof. Fortunate were the bystanders watching filming when Cage made one of his quick decisions, without forewarning, to cross the barrier, plunge into the crowd, and spend more time than ever expected signing autographs, shaking hands, and taking photos with fans and spectators, most of whom were left thrilled and stunned by the sudden contact.

Cage himself, having had much time to think about the character of Balthazar Blake while the film was developed over the span of many years, came to set with a crystalline notion of who the character was meant to be on-screen. "Balthazar Blake, along with Horvath and Veronica, was Merlin's apprentice," explains the actor. "After the evil Morgana rebels against Merlin, the three of us decide to use magic to try and protect mankind. Merlin casts a spell to keep us from aging for a thousand years, or until we find the Prime Merlinean, who is the inheritor of Merlin's power and is the one who will be able to save the world. Balthazar's job is to find him, which takes many centuries." The looking not only takes centuries, it spans the globe—from Old England to Calcutta in the nineteenth century. But for Balthazar, it is a journey that must be made, no matter the distance.

"The relationship between Balthazar and Dave is almost like a paternal one," Cage continues. "I think he may be the Prime Merlinean by virtue of the fact that he can wear Merlin's dragon ring, so when I find Dave, it's with great affection and relief. I want to guide him, instruct him, and train him for a larger purpose. But for Dave, it's pretty overwhelming to have someone walk into his life, tell him he's the descendent of Merlin, and that together we're going to save the world. If you're Dave, you're going to tell the guy he's nuts."

With the enormous weight of history riding on his shoulders—whether the Goethe poem, Dukas' tone poem, or Walt Disney's classic episode of *Fantasia*—was Nicolas Cage overwhelmed by the responsibility of starring in *The Sorcerer's Apprentice*? The actor replies with confidence but not a shred of arrogance. "Well, I wasn't. Because—and I say this with all honesty—I feel I'm the right person for this job. It all just feels right. It's the right group of people, the right time, and I feel that Walt Disney, somewhere, somehow, is with us on this one."

Cage was deeply attracted to one of the film's main themes, the meeting place between science (Dave's passion) and magic (Balthazar's vocation). "I'm one of those people who believes that the further you advance with science, the more it appears to be magic. There's a very fine line between the two. I mean, if you showed people the *Kitty Hawk* in flight in the year 500 AD, they would say it was magic. Well, it's science . . . but where do you really distinguish?"

FROM TOP: Balthazar Blake with his beloved Veronica (Monica Bellucci) during the Middle Ages; searching in India for the heir to Merlin; in battle mode at Bowling Green; with Dave (Jay Baruchel) in Washington Square Park.

Conjurers

"Nic doesn't try to make himself mysterious.
He actually *is* mysterious!"
—PRODUCTION CREW MEMBER

Jay Baruchel
Dave Stutler

COOL IS SPELLED "N-E-R-D"

"I'm a huge, huge nerd," confesses Jay Baruchel, immediately breaking the First Commandment of Young Leading Men ("Thou shalt not rep thyself as anything but the coolest dude on the planet"). "I love any movies where guys shoot energy out of their hands, but I'm not usually the go-to guy for stuff like that. They usually go for the Milo Ventimiglia type. And then I read this script, and I was like, wait a second . . . a guy like me gets to shoot energy out of his hands and stuff? Done! I'm here for the plasma bolts."

But let's get real—if Jay Baruchel is truly a nerd, and no one is arguing that he isn't, then he's also the coolest nerd in film today. This almost excessively talented young man, proudly hailing from Montreal, Canada, has demonstrated his acting chops in one role after another since he was twelve years old, including the leading role as very young lawyer Skip Ross in the Jerry Bruckheimer Television series *Just Legal*. "Jay has such wonderful comedic timing and is a brilliant verbal and physical performer," notes the producer, "and is such a unique actor. We think he's something special."

Jerry Bruckheimer shares that opinion with a host of other filmmakers, including the likes of Ben Stiller, Judd Apatow, Clint Eastwood, Lorene Scafaria, and Roger Avary, who have wisely cast Baruchel in their films, which have included *Tropic Thunder*, *Nick and Norah's Infinite Playlist*, *Knocked Up*, *Million Dollar Baby*, and *The Rules of Attraction*. Apatow first summoned Baruchel as one of the leads of his now-cult series *Undeclared*, and although the young veteran already had more than six years of professional experience before that point, it really served as his launching pad into the hearts and minds of audiences.

Says Jon Turteltaub, "Jay is just off-the-charts talented. Extremely smart, bold, funny, great with physical comedy. His body, mind, and voice all commit to whatever he's got to do. He doesn't have that silly "look at me" vanity that you get from a lot of funny people, it's much more intellectually thought out with Jay. He really looks for what's the story, what's the character, what's the essence, then finds the completely goofy, silly way of telling that story."

Nicolas Cage adds of his fellow star, "Jay is a really good person who's a lot of fun to be around. He has an inherent charm that comes out in his daily life and also on camera, and I think people are going to love watching him."

"I don't want to talk about Jay Baruchel," offers Alfred Molina with mock seriousness, "I want to beat him with a stick! Jay is seriously, for my money, one of the most talented young actors around at the moment. He's got great skills, great gifts. You know, he's still very young, but Jay has a real innate skill, and a confidence. I remember what I was like at that age, I didn't have a quarter of that confidence, of that sense of assuredness that he has, both as a person and as an actor.

"So I'm rather in awe of Jay, in a way," Molina continues. "You don't see the wheels going 'round, he makes it look easy. That's what makes really talented people watchable. I would say that

ABOVE: Costume illustrator Brian Valenzuela envisions Dave Stutler casting a shadow on the wall that holds an uncanny resemblance to the character's historic *Fantasia* ancestor.

"I've been tripping and falling down my whole life, so I figured that I might as well find a way to get paid for it."

—JAY BARUCHEL

Sinatra was a great singer because he made us all feel that we could do it. We all think that we sound like Sinatra when we're singing in the bath. Jay has that ease, that relaxation, and he's very inventive. When he has a chance to improvise on set, he's got great chops."

"Jay was a great surprise," proffers executive producer Chad Oman. "I knew he was funny . . . and he is very, *very* funny. What I didn't know is how good of a dramatic actor he is. He brought a tremendous amount of genuine emotion to the character. Jay made Dave very sympathetic by playing it real."

In addition to the appeal of shooting plasma out of his hands, Baruchel was seriously intrigued by Dave's character. "He's his own worst enemy, the architect of all his own misery," notes the actor with a laugh. "And I dug the arc that Dave goes on, it's a great hero's journey. Dave spends his life trying to live down that moment in the Arcana Cabana when he was ten years old and first encountered Balthazar Blake and Maxim Horvath. He gravitates toward physics, which is the discipline he gives his life to. When he meets up with Balthazar again, the sorcerer tells Dave that it was no coincidence that he drifted toward physics because although illusion and magic are different, magic and science are the same thing.

"Dave learns a lot about himself and affects changes," continues Baruchel, "and by the end of it, he's a full-blown sorcerer, the real deal. To be able to track from the kind of nerdy, nebbish guy to what Dave becomes was exciting for me. And I won't lie . . . the chance to get to do my own version of that most iconic of sequences—'The Sorcerer's Apprentice' episode from *Fantasia*—was a huge treat."

Despite his past success and enormous future, Jay Baruchel is a young man who exhibits an infectious enthusiasm, sense of humor, and complete lack of pretension, and is accessible and conversational with everyone on the crew, from way "above the line" to way below (especially if, true to the core of his Canadian roots, the subject was ice hockey and his beloved Montreal Canadiens). With an ever-present book—and never anything that could be described as beach reading—to keep him company during the camera setups and changeovers, and usually seen with a can of cola to keep him alert during the long shooting days, Baruchel's preternatural energy never flagged. Neither did his enthusiasm for the project. "This movie is going to blow people's minds, there's something to appeal to everyone. There are great fight scenes, chases, it's really, really funny, more than people might expect it to be. It's a big summer action movie. My point is, it'll be worth the twelve bucks!"

41

FROM TOP: Maxim Horvath (Alfred Molina) confronts Dave in an NYU washroom; Jay Baruchel, Teresa Palmer, and Ethan Peck shooting a scene on the NYU radio station set; Dave studies the fearsome Grimhold.

Conjurers

Alfred Molina
Maxim Horvath

GRAND VILLAINY

"I don't think I've ever had more fun working with an actor," states Jon Turteltaub in discussing Alfred Molina. "The first thing you learn is that he likes to be called 'Fred,' and that took a while because you're used to calling people by their name in the credits. But it's Fred Molina. Excuse me if I sound like I'm pretentiously inside by saying, 'Fred,' but that's how he's known to everybody. Fred shows up every day in a good mood and stays that way until he leaves. That lets you be in a good mood, and you can have fun and be creative. You want your villains to be attractive and charming, to fill the screen, and, boy, Fred is that guy."

It's not just director Jon Turteltaub and producer Jerry Bruckheimer who are members of Alfred Molina's admiration society. *Anyone* who has ever worked with Molina can attest to the undeniable fact that his enormous talents are only equaled by his luminous professionalism and great good humor. These traits, as everyone would be quick to agree, instantly leaven the on-set atmosphere with a buoyancy of spirit that helps even the most exhausted of cast and crew members make it to the end of yet another fifteen- or sixteen-hour day.

The irresistible combination of Alfred Molina's tremendous thespian skills, his versatility, and certainly his eternally positive attitude had to figure in why Jerry Bruckheimer invited the actor to segue almost immediately from portraying an amusingly shabby (but also slyly dangerous and potentially heroic) desert chieftain named Sheikh Amar in *Prince of Persia: The Sands of Time* to the urbane, sophisticated, and often terrifying Maxim Horvath in *The Sorcerer's Apprentice*. "Alfred Molina is a wonderful actor, somebody who can give any role an unexpected twist, and humor as well," notes Bruckheimer.

"Alfred Molina is one of those actors that, every time he's in a movie, he's doing something totally different," comments Turteltaub. "You can't believe he's the same guy you saw in the other movie, or the play. He's always different. He also has an unbelievably light touch and fun sense of humor. Fred is a very playful guy, and I think we see that impishness in the character of Horvath, as well as bringing the gravity that the character needs. There's nothing more frightening in a villain than intelligence. You know you can defeat power and strength, but it's really hard to outsmart someone who's really intelligent. Fred brings that air of power and sense of villainy that doesn't feel false. He can make you feel and understand Horvath's anger . . . and cruelty."

"Alfred Molina is one of the funniest persons I've ever met in my life," notes Teresa Palmer somewhat ironically, since Molina portrays a character who absolutely terrorizes her throughout the film. "You can't help but be in a good mood around Fred, because he's got such a bubbly, wonderful energy that he brings to the set every day."

As for Molina himself, he was good to go from the first time he heard about the role of Horvath. "As I was completing *Prince of Persia*, which was such a good experience, somebody told me that I was being considered for the role, and would I be interested? I sort of tried to play cool, debonair, and

ABOVE: **Conceptual illustration by Gregory Hill of Horvath's layer of the Grimhold.**

44

nonchalant, but I ended up showing heaves of chalant. I was fascinated by the fact that they were including elements of the classic 'Sorcerer's Apprentice' episode from *Fantasia*, and really liked the character once I read the script.

"It seemed a million miles away from what I'd done in *Prince of Persia*," Molina recollects. "Sheikh Amar was a conniving, opportunistic sort of rogue, while Horvath is a rather smart, debonair, Edwardian villain. A villain whom I regard as being in the classic tradition of suave bad guys, well dressed, charming but deadly. I thought of all the British actors over the years who have played such parts in American films, and I suddenly thought that by playing Horvath I actually belong to an honorable tradition going right back to people like Basil Rathbone."

If any man might be granted the right of way to arrogance, then by all rights Alfred Molina, with a stupendous body of work of more than seventy film, television, and theater productions behind him, *should* be gazing down from lofty heights with an occasional nod to the masses below. But that's not the way he rolls. "You've got to take it all with a pinch of salt," he says of his profession. "I mean, it's important, but it's not brain surgery. You know, we're making movies. It's part of the magic, and that's the best thing."

The London-born Molina has now been on-screen for nearly thirty years, since making his feature film debut as Indiana Jones' duplicitous South American guide in *Raiders of the Lost Ark*, in 1981. His motion picture credits since then have included films both independent and commercial, of every genre, and roles of every nature: just a sampling includes *Prick Up Your Ears*, *Not Without My Daughter*, *Enchanted April*, *Maverick*, Paul Thomas Anderson's *Boogie Nights* and *Magnolia*, *Chocolat*, Julie Taymor's *Frida* (in which his performance as artist Diego Rivera won him numerous Best Supporting Actor nominations, including one from the British Academy of Film and Television Arts), *Spider-Man 2* (in which he won major genre street cred as Doc Ock), and *The Da Vinci Code*. Most recently, Molina has received rave reviews for his performance in Lone Scherfig's *An Education*, and portrays Stephano in Julie Taymor's *The Tempest*. Onstage, he received Tony Award nominations for *Fiddler on the Roof* (as Tevye the Milkman in the classic musical) and Yasmina Reza's *Art*, winning both the Drama Desk and Outer Circle Critics Awards for the latter.

So this is obviously a man who gets to know his on-screen alter egos and finds something to empathize with. "In *The Sorcerer's Apprentice*, Horvath's mission is world domination, which is some-thing I share with the character," says Molina, tongue planted firmly in cheek. "Balthazar and Horvath have a rivalry that's gone on for millennia. They were once very close friends and disciples of Merlin, but an event occurred a thousand years ago sending Horvath in the opposite direction from his former allies. Balthazar is maintaining the Merlinean standard of magic as a power that's used for the benefit of mankind. Horvath is the leader of the Morganians, who take the very different view that magic should be used to subjugate humans. That's the struggle between good as personified by Nic Cage's character, and evil as personified by mine."

Luckily for all those who work with Molina, there is no evil to be found. And when on the rare occasion things do get tense? "I just go to craft service," the actor notes with eyebrows half-raised.

FROM TOP: The many faces of Alfred Molina as Maxim Horvath. With sorcerer's cane; acting opposite the illusionist Drake Stone (Toby Kebbell); being filmed by a Steadicam operator; having a laugh on set.

Part III

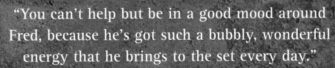

"You can't help but be in a good mood around Fred, because he's got such a bubbly, wonderful energy that he brings to the set every day."

—TERESA PALMER

Teresa Palmer
Becky Barnes

BEAUTY, BRAINS, AND BACKBONE

It seems improbable that the almost impossibly lovely Teresa Palmer—she of the perfect bone structure, radiant blue eyes, and shimmering blond hair—could also be as down-home, hardworking, personable, and just plain nice as she actually is. But this is not an illusion, that's exactly what Teresa Palmer is, in addition to being impeccably professional, talented, and devoted to her craft of acting. A relatively recent arrival from Adelaide, Australia, Palmer—known to friends and colleagues as Tez—imbues her role of Becky Barnes, the seemingly unreachable object of Dave Stutler's ten-year-long desire, with equal measures of beauty, brains, and backbone.

Although *The Sorcerer's Apprentice* represents the first time that Palmer has worked on a Jerry Bruckheimer production, it was her second feature for Walt Disney Pictures. "I initially heard about the project through my manager just after I finished shooting *Bedtime Stories* for Disney," recollects Palmer, who portrayed Violet Nottingham in the film, which starred Adam Sandler. "When he told me that the film was loosely based on the segment of *Fantasia*, I got very excited, because I'm a huge fan of that film. I auditioned a couple of times for Jerry Bruckheimer and Jon Turteltaub, and found out the day after *Bedtime Stories* premiered that I got the role.

"My character is Becky," explains Palmer, "an NYU student who had gone to school with Jay Baruchel's character, Dave, ten years before. He always had a crush on Becky, but she considered him more of a friend. They run into each other at NYU, where Dave is also a student, and they spark up this connection again. Dave still has his thing for Becky, but she's a little bit wary, but slowly starts to notice what a wonderful and endearing person Dave is."

But challenges, as they must, soon present themselves to Dave and Becky. First in the form of a dashingly handsome D.J. at the radio station named Andre (played by Ethan Peck, whose dark good looks not so coincidentally echo those of his esteemed grandfather, Gregory Peck) and then in the form of Balthazar Blake. Entering Dave's life, Blake is set on the path of not only training him to be a sorcerer, but, well, saving the world. This obviously complicates Dave's relationship with Becky. "I think that Becky stands in for the audience because, like them, she doesn't have any experience with magic and the world of sorcery, and can't wrap her head around it when Dave explains who he is and what he has to do. It's a fine line between Becky being in total shock and very scared. Eventually, she sort of starts to become excited by this world of sorcery, and by that stage, the audience is in that place too."

For the coveted role of Becky, the filmmakers had little doubt that Teresa Palmer was a perfect fit. "Teresa is somebody who we've liked for a long time," notes Jerry Bruckheimer, "and she did a fantastic job auditioning with Jay. When you have that magic between two actors, you've got to cast them together." Confirms Jon Turteltaub, "Tez is just that person who walks into a room and it feels like someone turned the lights on. It always seems the hardest part of casting is finding an

"Tez is just that person who walks into a room and it feels like someone turned the lights on."

—JON TURTELTAUB

actress who is movie-star beautiful, movie-star charming, with genuine acting ability. That's already a miracle. But one who's funny? Impossible. Then in walks this girl who is jaw-droppingly pretty, has an inviting warmth about her, a lack of arrogance and fear, but without standoffishness. And you can see why Dave would be in love with her. Tez is a joy."

"There's a lack of misery to [Becky]," Turteltaub continues, "and that's the thing Dave needs in his life, to get out of that intellectual anger and that college angst, and have some joy and fresh air. Unlike every other actress who came in for the role looking for Becky's angry side, Tez came in and looked for the joyous side, and, boy, that was just really infectious."

Palmer was indeed joyous about landing the role of Becky. "I still don't think it's really sunk in that I'm doing a Jerry Bruckheimer film," she exclaimed midway through the shoot. "*Pirates of the Caribbean* is one of my favorite movies of all time, and I'm still pinching myself!"

"I have to say that on days when we're shooting the scenes in which Teresa has to pretend to like me as Dave, it doesn't suck to be me at all," laughs Jay Baruchel. "Teresa and I have known each other for a while, so we were friends going into the movie. She's sweet and funny and adorable, just comes in and makes everyone happier whenever she's around. And she's also one heck of an actress."

Teresa Palmer first caught the attention of worldwide audiences with her leading role as a high school student with a dark secret in the Australian independent film *2:37*, which screened at both the Cannes Film Festival and the Toronto Film Festival. Palmer received a nomination from the Australian Film Institute for her work, and was named as one of Australia's "Stars of Tomorrow" by *Screen International* magazine. She quickly followed with a costarring role opposite Sarah Michelle Gellar and Jennifer Beals in Japanese director Takashi Shimizu's *The Grudge 2*, and starring roles opposite Daniel Radcliffe in the coming-of-age story *December Boys* and the psychological thriller *Restraint*. Not surprisingly, the United States and Walt Disney Pictures then came calling with *Bedtime Stories*, which Palmer followed by starring opposite Anna Faris and Topher Grace in the Universal Pictures/Imagine Entertainment film *Kids in America*.

For *The Sorcerer's Apprentice*, Teresa Palmer not only had to perfect her American accent, but also had to make sure that she kept clear of the explosions. "This is the first film in which I've had to deal with a lot of special effects, so it's been interesting to try and balance it all, like concentrating on the work, the accent, and hitting specific marks because something's gonna burst into flames," she explains. "You can feel that you're part of a huge movie, and it's just so exciting."

FROM TOP: Becky (Teresa Palmer) and Andre (Ethan Peck) in the radio station studio; Teresa Palmer is given the honor of holding the camera clapper board before a take; Dave and Becky ride in the Rolls-Royce Phantom.

Conjurers

49

Monica Bellucci
Veronica

PURE CLASS

For generations, cinephiles have been grateful to Italy for providing the film world with some of the most enduringly talented, soulful, and beautiful actresses in the history of the medium: think Sophia Loren, Anna Magnani, Silvana Mangano, Claudia Cardinale, Gina Lollobrigida, and Isabella Rossellini, just to name a few. One of the few Italian contemporaries who can make a claim to such celebrated company is Monica Bellucci, who in film after film, on both sides of the Atlantic, has exuded not only pure class, but also considerable versatility. Effortlessly shifting genres and even languages (she has spoken Italian, French, English, and even the ancient tongue of Aramaic for her roles), she now graces *The Sorcerer's Apprentice* by performing in the extremely challenging role of Veronica, the medieval sorceress who, to a large degree, is at the very heart of the story.

"We were so fortunate to land Monica for the film," says Jerry Bruckheimer. "She's a huge star in Europe, but has also done really great work in American films as well. The part of Veronica needed someone who can make the audience understand why and how Balthazar can have a love and devotion that has lasted for more than a thousand years."

"Who's the right actress to play someone worth waiting a thousand years for?" questions Jon Turteltaub. "She sure better be pretty and special. She better be age-appropriate, because if you're fortysomething, and you waited all this time for someone who's still nineteen, you're creepy. You need for him to be waiting for a woman, not a girl, who has strength. We looked around the world for that woman, and luckily, we got Monica Bellucci. She's got that Italian power, which is sexy and strong, and she knows what you're thinking before you're thinking it. Monica is also a sweetheart, lovely, fun, a great mom. But you've got to get over the first bit of being intimidated by the most powerful, beautiful woman you've ever met. . . ." Turteltaub stops and then adds, "After my wife."

As for Jay Baruchel, he was just happy to be working with fellow artists who fulfilled his fondest career hopes. "Monica Bellucci has starred in some of my favorite films of all time, she's probably the most beautiful woman in the history of the world, and I can't believe I was lucky enough to work with her. There was one night when both Monica and Teresa Palmer were working at the same time, and I thought, *this* is why I got into acting!"

Bellucci had her own thoughts of the role going into it. "Veronica is the long-lost love of Balthazar Blake," explains the stunning native of Citta di Castello, Umbria, in her perfect, if charmingly accented, English. "And in the film, I sometimes have to play a double role, because there are scenes in which Veronica is possessed by the evil sorceress Morgana. That's why I wanted to be part of this project, because it was interesting to have the chance to play a double personality . . . and also to make a film that my five-year-old daughter, Deva, can watch."

The actress was also drawn to *The Sorcerer's Apprentice* by the cast already in place. "I respect Nicolas Cage very much as an actor and also as a person," she comments, "because he's very nice,

ABOVE: Gregory Hill brings Veronica's strength and beauty to life in this early drawing.

very open, and very generous to work with. I enjoy very much working with Alfred Molina, an amazing actor with a great sense of humor. Jay Baruchel is full of energy, so young, so original, and spontaneous. And I love to work with Jon Turteltaub, because he gives me the freedom to explore different acting choices, but at the same time knows what he wants. I feel safe because of that."

From Monica Bellucci's point of view, *The Sorcerer's Apprentice* is a love story. "Balthazar and Veronica are willing to do everything for their love, and at the same time they're two fighters. Horvath, who, like them, is a disciple of Merlin, also falls in love with Veronica. She rejects him for Balthazar, and because of that he betrays them by aligning himself with Morgana. It's a beautiful and powerful story about love, jealousy, and vengeance."

Beautiful is definitely an apt adjective to describe Monica Bellucci and her screen presence. But it is not the only one. Powerful and intelligent also work well and her professional background speaks volumes about her multilayered talent. Originally set on a career in law, she began modeling at the age of sixteen to pay her tuition at the University of Perugia, and was photographed by a number of the world's greatest photographers, among them Richard Avedon, Bruce Weber, and Helmut Newton. After modeling for some time, Bellucci sought to expand her artistic expression into acting. She made her screen debut as one of the brides of *Bram Stoker's Dracula* in Francis Ford Coppola's 1992 film. This was the starting point for a quickly burgeoning screen career that saw Bellucci accepting major roles in films both in Europe (*Malena*; *Brotherhood of the Wolf*; *Remember Me*; *My Love*; *The Stone Council*; *Don't Look Back*, *Baaria*) and the United States (*Under Suspicion*, *Tears of the Sun*, Persephone in the Wachowski Brothers' *The Matrix Reloaded* and *The Matrix Revolutions*, Mary Magdalene in Mel Gibson's *The Passion of the Christ*, Spike Lee's *She Hate Me*, The Mirror Queen in Terry Gilliam's *The Brothers Grimm*, and *The Lives of Pippa Lee*).

Bellucci finds no contradiction between these two distinct branches of her artistic life, "art" films in Europe and more commercial fare in the United States, and certainly makes no apologies for enjoying both. "Actually, it's great for me to have the chance to come here once in a while and make American movies."

The actress sums this experience up perfectly by saying, "In *The Sorcerer's Apprentice*, audiences are going to find everything: a love story, mystery, danger, humor, and magic. And it's also a movie for everybody, children and adults alike. It's everybody's fantasy to have magic powers."

FROM TOP: Veronica and Balthazar in medieval England; Balthazar catches a fleeting glimpse of his beloved Veronica on New York's Sixth Avenue . . . which turns out to be a trick of the eye devised by rival Maxim Horvath; Balthazar and Veronica reunite to battle the forces of evil in Bowling Green.

"The part of Veronica needed someone who can make the audience understand why and how Balthazar can have a love and devotion that has lasted for more than a thousand years."

—JERRY BRUCKHEIMER

Toby Kebbell
Drake Stone

THE MORGANIAN PUNK

Alfred Molina wasn't the only actor to make the quick trek from the deserts of Morocco and the soundstages of Pinewood Studios for *Prince of Persia: The Sands of Time* to the contemporary city-scape of New York for *The Sorcerer's Apprentice*. Toby Kebbell was also enlisted to shift his talents from one epic Jerry Bruckheimer production to another. And just as Molina's character of Maxim Horvath in the latter provided a startling contrast to the one he portrayed in the former, so was Kebbell's versatility called into play. In *Prince of Persia*, the actor is seen as Garsiv, the warlike brother of Dastan, the title character portrayed by Jake Gyllenhaal. Those seeing Kebbell as Garsiv, always in armor, with beard and long hair giving him an imposingly rough-hewn aspect, would barely recognize him as the long, lean, punked-out illusionist Drake Stone, with his two-tone hair, goatee, and flamboyant, skintight clothes.

But that's the nature of Toby Kebbell. A relentlessly creative young talent, he has an intensity leavened by considerable and often highly irreverent (but good-natured) humor. In his relatively brief career he has already proven that variety is definitely the spice of life. "Toby is just loaded with energy," says Jerry Bruckheimer, "and he's the kind of actor who always surprises because you never, ever know what he's going to do next."

"Toby is a chameleon," adds executive producer Chad Oman. "We had just finished working with him on *Prince of Persia*. There were several crew members on *The Sorcerer's Apprentice* who also worked on *Persia*, and none of them recognized Toby when he came to set dressed as Drake Stone. Originally, the Drake character was very small and had almost no dialogue, but Toby is so good and brought so much personality to the character that we gave him a lot more dialogue and screen time. He brought the perfect amount of bluster and strength to his role."

It didn't take Toby Kebbell very long to think about whether or not he wanted to join *The Sorcerer's Apprentice* company after he got the offer from Bruckheimer and Turteltaub to take on the character of Drake Stone, the ego-driven illusionist with a huge following, but with no fan bigger than himself. "Drake Stone is a modern-day alt-illusionist who is actually a sorcerer," says Kebbell. "He's the kind of guy who wanted to make a lot of money, get famous, and kiss a lot of girls. The fact that Drake is a sorcerer with mystical powers was really exciting to me. I knew that I would get to create lightning bolts out of my hand and drive Ferraris through Times Square. It was a challenge to show off another eccentricity of my ability . . . my own innate sense of lunacy."

Explains Alfred Molina, "In the course of the story I need to enlist the help of an ally. I skirt the city for various malevolent contacts, and I'm pointed in the direction of a Morganian named Drake Stone. We discover that at a very young age, he was abandoned by his mentor, a sorcerer who taught him his skills, so he decides to use them as an entertainer. Horvath despises that. He feels that Drake sold out and uses his sorcery for cheap thrills. He turns into a frustrating ally, but eventually

ABOVE: Dean Tschetter's portrait of Drake Stone reveals the illusionist in all his pomp and glory.

"Toby is just loaded with energy, and he's the kind of actor who always surprises because you never, ever know what he's going to do next."

—JERRY BRUCKHEIMER

gets in Horvath's way. I think of the relationship between Maxim and Drake as a kind of dysfunctional family, like a really overbearing father and a son who's turned out to be a huge disappointment."

Toby Kebbell may indeed have an innate sense of lunacy, but if so, it goes part and parcel with an innate talent that has won him considerable attention from filmmakers and audiences in a very short time. The young native of Pontecraft, North Yorkshire, Kebbell was by his own description a tough kid growing up in the hardscrabble north of England who was saved by a growing passion for acting. Attending the Central Television Workshop in Nottinghamshire, Kebbell's youthful skills were noticed by filmmaker Shane Meadows, whose independent feature-film chronicles of British working-class life in the Midlands had developed a devoted following. Meadows cast Kebbell as Paddy Considine's mentally challenged brother in *Dead Man's Shoes*, which brought him a British Independent Film Award (BIFA) nomination as Best Newcomer.

Kebbell was then cast by Oliver Stone in a small but pivotal role in *Alexander*, which led to a role in the West End production of *Journey's End* and Michael Attenborough's production of *Enemies* at the famed Almeida Theater in Islington. Kebbell then returned to features in Anton Corbijn's acclaimed *Control*, portraying Rob Gretton in the screen biography of Joy Division's Ian Curtis. For that role he received a BIFA for Best Supporting Actor. Continuing his choice of fearless roles, Kebbell went on to portray the decidedly troubled rocker Johnny Quid in Guy Ritchie's *RocknRolla*, winning him yet more acclaim. It was then that Hollywood, as manifested by Jerry Bruckheimer and director Mike Newell, came knocking for *Prince of Persia: The Sands of Time*.

Kebbell has garnered fans not just from the world of audiences and critics, but his fellow artists as well. "He's got this inherent kind of unusual energy, charm, and humor about him," notes Nicolas Cage. Recalls Alfred Molina, "Although Toby and I didn't actually have any scenes together in *Prince of Persia*, because his story line was running parallel to mine, we spent a lot of time together on location in Morocco on our days off. So in *The Sorcerer's Apprentice*, it's been a nice opportunity to redress the balance a little bit. We've had lots of good, juicy scenes together, and it's been great fun. Toby is seriously gifted and, like Jay, is like a duck to water with improvisation."

Kebbell definitely enjoyed the physical transformation he underwent to become Drake. "The look for this character is certainly fantastic," he enthuses, "thanks to our great costume designer, Michael Kaplan; makeup artist, Bernadette Mazur; and hair department head, Alan D'Angerio. One of the beautiful things about doing this film is that they let you come up with a hundred ideas, and then they refine them to what's practical and possible. I told Michael that I'd love for Drake to have a big, long coat, and he instantly added his own brilliance to that concept. And heeled boots, which if you wear, you've lost your mind. Then, to make Drake look even more ridiculous, I wanted one of those terrible beards that, unless you're a jazz musician, you should be ashamed of yourself for having. And silly, repulsive hair.

"What I like about playing Drake," concludes Toby Kebbell, "is that it's nice to get the arrogance and pomposity that I might not have in myself out in a character in a creative way. Drake Stone is a jerk, and it's always fun to play one, rather than *be* one!"

Omar Benson Miller
Bennett

BIG MAN, BIG HEART

Omar Benson Miller, all eminently lovable six feet six inches of him, takes a break from filming while standing next to one of the rusting generators on the massive underground lab found inside the Bedford Armory. "Bennett is not only Dave Stutler's roommate," notes Miller of the character he embodies in *The Sorcerer's Apprentice*, "but also his motivator. He's one of the many people in the film, like Balthazar Blake and Becky Barnes, who are trying to get Dave up and at 'em, making him more *pro*active in his life, and less *re*active. I try to teach him the importance of going after things, including the girl he's in love with, his magic, his sorcery, and his studies.

"The genius of the way that Bennett is written," Miller continues, "is that it shows that people come from all walks of life, and they can do anything. That's what we're trying to get Dave to understand, that just because he's the smart guy, it doesn't mean he has to be scared to talk to the girl. Be who you are, wear it proudly, stick your chest out, and say, 'Hey, this is me!'"

And with that, Miller lets loose one of his highly contagious laughs, a sound one often hears from this very accomplished young actor whose gusto for life seems to echo Bennett's. And why not? The Los Angeles native has made quite an impression on audiences and filmmakers, first coming to prominence as Sol George, one of Eminem's homeboys in Curtis Hanson's acclaimed *8 Mile*. Roles followed in such films as *Shall We Dance*, *Get Rich or Die Tryin'*, Hanson's *Lucky You*, and *Things We Lost in the Fire*. Miller was then cast by director Spike Lee as Private First Class Sam Train in his World War II epic *Miracle at St. Anna*, which was filmed on location in Italy. Miller has also been a fixture on Jerry Bruckheimer's network TV shows, as a regular on both *Eleventh Hour* and, most recently, *CSI: Miami*. In addition, he enjoyed guest appearances on *The West Wing* and *Karen Sisco*, among others.

Miller clearly had a good time working with Nicolas Cage and Jay Baruchel on *The Sorcerer's Apprentice*. "Cool recognizes cool," he says of a scene in which Balthazar and Bennett hit it off, much to Dave's annoyance. "Balthazar shows up out of nowhere and introduces himself as Dave's uncle. I like his style, I like his clothes, and little do I know that he's just come out of medieval times. It's great working with Nic. You know, he's one of the most famous people in the world, and one of the best actors, yet he walks on set as humble as anyone else. And this movie will show off Jay Baruchel's talents to the world on a very grand stage."

Then he smiles. "And it's great to be in the Jerry Bruckheimer family, because he's so loyal to his performers and creates high-quality content the whole family can enjoy."

For Omar Benson Miller—with a cinematic family that includes names like Jerry Bruckheimer, Spike Lee, Curtis Hanson, and Jon Turteltaub—if there's any better way to work, it hasn't yet been invented.

FROM TOP: Omar Benson Miller exhibits a wide range of expressions as the ebullient Bennett.

Conjurers

MANIFESTATIONS

Duel in the Arcana Cabana

THE SCENE: The first action set piece of *The Sorcerer's Apprentice* is a spectacular sorcerer's duel between archenemies Balthazar Blake (Nicolas Cage) and Maxim Horvath (Alfred Molina) in the Arcana Cabana. This decidedly bizarre old curiosity shop in Lower Manhattan belongs to Blake who has over the long years filled its spooky confines to the rafters with all manner of bric-a-brac.

When the scene opens, ten-year-old Dave Stutler (Jake Cherry) has been lured away from his class on a school trip by a runaway love note he penned to young Becky Blake (Peyton Roi List). His chase leads him into the Arcana Cabana, where he first encounters the enigmatic and intimidating Balthazar. Coincidence or magic? Once again, the answer is a resounding yes. After the powerful dragon ring (it once belonged to Merlin himself) literally walks onto young Dave's finger and settles there, Balthazar informs him that he's the one he's been searching for for hundreds of years. Balthazar goes on to tell Dave that he is going to be a very important sorcerer. But when Dave accidentally releases Balthazar's archenemy Maxim Horvath from the Grimhold, the ensuing battle of opposing magical forces is terrifying enough to send the boy escaping back into the safer streets of Manhattan.

BEHIND THE SCENE: At some point during the course of any production there's a moment when the cast and crew, having labored long and hard, come

ABOVE: Asylum Visual Effects images of the dragon ring as it magically wraps itself around young Dave's finger. OPPOSITE: A gargoyle looms over the Manhattan exterior of the Arcana Cabana in this composite illustration by Gregory Hill (Arcana Cabana) and Tani Kunitake (gargoyle).

to recognize that the discombobulated and disjointed bits and shards of film that have gone into the camera have actually coagulated into something resembling a real movie. For the company of *The Sorcerer's Apprentice*, that welcome epiphany occurred on Tuesday, May 19, 2009, the fifty-third of eighty-eight days of principal photography.

It happened, of all places, in a men's room. Well, actually, it was a set, a men's room created especially for the movie at Steiner Studios in Brooklyn. So both men and women crammed themselves into a relatively tight space to watch a preliminary edit of a scene that had been shot two months (and forty-nine shooting

days) earlier, in which ten-year-old Dave Stutler first encounters sorcerer Balthazar Blake in the delicious spooky interior of the Arcana Cabana and watches with rising increments of fascination and horror as Blake engages in magical combat with rival sorcerer and archenemy Maxim Horvath. Although the edit was still rough, with visible green screen, wires, cables, and a stunt player in green tights wielding a sword—all of which would be digitally "painted out" later—the company was riveted to the monitor in "video village." Laughter alternated with gasps, and in the end, the group burst into applause, much to the pleasure of producer Jerry Bruckheimer and director Jon Turteltaub. Movie crews are notoriously the toughest critics of all.

With so much complex shooting yet to be done, it was the proverbial shot in the arm that the company needed, the moment when all of the work, all of the long hours, all of the exacting effort had become, well, *magical*. And even for the grizzled and veteran company, that's what their work is supposed to be all about.

"I saw the Arcana Cabana scene as the overture for the rest of the movie," notes Turteltaub. "We see the history, and the kind of magic that will be displayed throughout the film. The relationship between Balthazar and Dave is established, and we know from that scene what the rest of the movie will be in terms of tone, emotion, drama, action, and effects."

The Arcana Cabana battle is the first time we witness sorcery in action in the film. Starting from when Merlin's dragon ring very magically comes to life and walks onto Dave's finger, it then moves to

63

Director of photography Bojan Bazelli (right) and camera operator Mark Schmidt examine items on the Arcana Cabana set at Steiner Studios in Brooklyn.

Horvath's emergence from the Grimhold (which would delight the most avid entomologists). "The Grimhold," explains Nicolas Cage, "is a prison for the very, very scary and wicked Morganians, and the more evil the Morganian, the deeper into the circles of this sort of Russian nesting doll they go. Morgana is in the center. The obstacle is that it keeps getting taken, and every time that happens, Horvath has the ability to open it and release another very dangerous force of Morganian evil."

The magic then speeds on as Balthazar and Horvath use the full range of their powers to cast spells, move objects, and, in essence, blow the place to bits before they're both—finally—sucked into a

large urn. There they will remain until both reemerge into each other's (and Dave's) lives in another decade.

The Arcana Cabana sequence provides a perfect example of how interdepartmental cooperation was essential to creating a compelling and believable sequence. As with every other foot of film, the scene combined the efforts of director Jon Turteltaub along with the other magicians of *The Sorcerer's Apprentice*, his key creative team. The team included many, such as masterful director of photography Bojan Bazelli (*Hairspray*), who had already shot *G-Force* for Jerry Bruckheimer (and who the producer describes as "a true artist"). Bazelli's quest for new imagery led him to be the first of his profession to use a brand-new film stock from Kodak just out of the lab and not even yet available for commercial consumption. Production designer Naomi Shohan, acclaimed for her work on such films as *Constantine* and *I Am Legend*, was also part of the team, along with costume designer Michael Kaplan, who had worked on Bruckheimer films, from *Flashdance*, in 1983, to *Pearl Harbor*, nearly twenty years later. In addition to the designers, the creative team included innovative Academy Award–winning visual-effects supervisor John Nelson (*Gladiator*); legendary special-effects supervisor John Frazier (who received Academy Award nominations for Jerry Bruckheimer's productions *Armageddon*, *Pearl Harbor*, and *Pirates of the Caribbean: At World's End*, and took home the award for *Spider-Man 2*), and his on-set coordinator Mark Hawker; as well as stunt coordinator George Marshall Ruge (*Pirates of the Caribbean* and *Lord of the Rings* trilogies, and both *National Treasure* films), who executive producer Mike Stenson calls "the best in the world at what he does." And then there were the

ABOVE: Spooky seventeenth-century witch Abigail Williams (Nicole Ehinger) and a Gregory Hill illustration of her layer of the Grimhold. BOTTOM LEFT: Horvath Grimhold concepts by Gregory Hill. OPPOSITE: Gregory Hill's illustration of production designer Naomi Shohan's richly evocative Arcana Cabana interior.

remarkably talented makeup and hair departments, under department heads Bernadette Mazur and Alan D'Angerio, respectively, with Nicolas Cage's longtime hair/makeup artist Ilona Herman transforming him on a daily basis into a sorcerer whose look would be equally acceptable in the eleventh and twenty-first centuries.

For the sequence, Shohan created a remarkable set that was not only richly detailed and atmospheric, but also a fabulous playing field for the mayhem that would soon ensue. "The main reason we had to build that extraordinary set," notes Turteltaub, "is that you can't go to some store and say, 'Do you mind if we

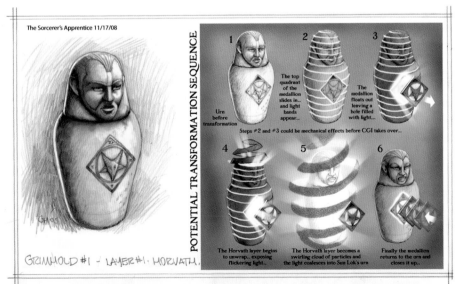

The Sorcerer's Apprentice 11/17/08

POTENTIAL TRANSFORMATION SEQUENCE

GRIMHOLD #1 - LAYER #1 - HORVATH.

Urn before transformation

1. The top quadrant of the medallion slides in... and light bands appear...
2. The medallion floats out leaving a hole filled with light...
3.

Steps #2 and #3 could be mechanical effects before CGI takes over...

4. The Horvath layer begins to unwrap... exposing flickering light...
5. The Horvath layer becomes a swirling cloud of particles and the light coalesces into Sun Lok's urn...
6. Finally the medallion returns to the urn and closes it up...

have people flying around, set fires, and ruin all of your antiques?' Instead, Naomi designed a set that was huge, awesome, ominous, and scary, but also practical so that the stunt team could rig wires so that people could fly to the ceiling, and build a fake ceiling so that an actor doesn't have to be stuck upside down on a real ceiling for four hours."

"This scene establishes the magic that sorcerers are capable of doing," says John Nelson. "We see plasma generated and fired for the first time. Fires are created through pyrokinesis. There are concussion blasts, matter is moved through telekinesis, and there's a gravity inversion spell by Balthazar that sends Horvath hurtling up to the ceiling. It's a true collaborative effort of practical effects, stunts, the actors, camera, direction, everybody together to really make it go."

Nelson goes on to explain his philosophy: "We do visual effects for things that are either too dangerous, too expensive, or impossible to do. My idea of a perfect visual effect is one that starts with a practical effect, say, a real event that can be photographed, and then goes into something that's amazing that looks real, ending with another practical effect. We

have a great group of people under physical-effects supervisor John Frazier working on set, including Mark Hawker, Eric Rylander, Jimmy Nagel, and the others, and they're terrific at providing what's known as 'floor effects' to make everything as real as possible. Then we go and take it someplace else."

"Since the advent of computer-generated images, you read scripts and hope that you can get 25 percent of the effects that are required," confesses John Frazier. "But the great thing is, we're either going to take the lead into a gag, or do the final, and somewhere in there there's going to be this really great mix of CGI and live mechanical effects. That's the way Jon Turteltaub likes the shoot. He wants as much of it live as possible, and then enhance it with CGI. Audiences are now so sophisticated, they don't want to see stuff like what we did in the sixties and seventies that was totally mechanical. But on the other hand, sometimes when something is done entirely CGI, it looks like a cartoon rather than a movie.

"We did a lot of live effects on *The Sorcerer's Apprentice*," continues Frazier. "Our guys worked for weeks on developing different colored fires and smokes that are nonetheless environmentally correct.

Magic has always been about smoke and mirrors, and we have *both* in the movie!"

The Arcana Cabana sequence also presented stunt coordinator George Marshall Ruge and his team, including longtime assistant stunt coordinator Dan Barringer and head stunt rigger Kurt Lott, with their first opportunity to shine. "George Ruge is without question one of the premier stunt people of all time," enthuses Turteltaub. "He seems to refuse to do unsuccessful movies, which is why I really like him. I think he's a good-luck charm. George is the sweetest guy in the world, but he runs his ship like a tough drill sergeant where everybody is doing exactly what they need to do because with him, safety is everything. George also really cares about story more than the stunt, so he studies the characters, and what's more, so do the stunt doubles he employs." In the case of *The Sorcerer's Apprentice*, when a stunt was just too dangerous to allow the leading players to do it themselves, it meant that Thomas Dupont, Dan Brown, and Rob Mars were on point to double as Balthazar, Dave, and Horvath.

"The first fight in the Arcana Cabana not only sets the tone, but also introduces the three main characters

TOP: In this image from Double Negative Visual Effects, Balthazar forms a powerful plasma ball in the underground lab where he trains Dave. ABOVE: Academy Award–winning visual-effects supervisor John Nelson on the Arcana Cabana set at Steiner Studios.

Stunt coordinator George Marshall Ruge (left) works on the Chinatown sequence on Eldridge Street.

of the movie," notes Ruge, "so it was really important to me to work out the details. And even though we did plenty of wire and other stunt work, it was all very character-driven. And in the course of things we have people flying around, hitting walls, hand-to-hand combat, and a magical sword fight between a disembodied sword being controlled by Horvath versus Balthazar Blake using a unicorn horn."

"I couldn't believe we started off with that huge fight scene," recalls Alfred Molina. "I always have this notion that when you start work on a film, there'll be a couple of nice, easy days. You'll get to know everybody, sit around, have a couple of cups of coffee, chat away, and do some nice, simple little scene. For this, I went straight into rehearsals for the Arcana Cabana sequence. I'd barely had time to unpack, and suddenly I had a magic cane in one hand and a sword in the

other, going at it with Nic. It was a bit of a shock, but it was great to start out with all systems going."

"We sent Horvath flying up about twenty-seven feet to the ceiling of the Arcana Cabana on a cable," notes Ruge, "and Fred was very game for that. We also did what we call a 'double ratchet,' in which Balthazar and Horvath blast each other diagonally across the room, one into a pillar and one back by the stairs. Because the set was so confined and cluttered, I had a lot of concerns about fitting the action in here, but it worked out OK."

"George Marshall Ruge is absolutely fantastic," says Molina, "very imaginative and interesting. He likes to think of stunt work as choreography, which I think is a really good way of looking at it. George says that the moment of impact is not what's important. What's important is the buildup to it, and the reaction from it. And of course, he's right, because that's where all the drama is."

Special-effects foreman Mark Hawker and his team utilized a plethora of techniques for various parts of the overall Arcana Cabana sequence, which in their parlance are referred to as "gags." "When young Dave puts on the magical dragon ring, he accidentally makes the Grimhold break through from behind the wall," explains Hawker. "We took the Grimhold and

put it on an eight-foot stick with swivels on both ends. So wherever Dave moves his hand, the Grimhold follows, and it keeps that distance. Of course, John Nelson's team will 'paint' out the stick with computers. We had lots of breakaway walls and furniture, and when Horvath gets pulled up into the skylight by one of Balthazar's spells, we used a rubber skylight with breakaway glass.

"There's also a moment where Horvath has a fire in his hand, and he's throwing all these spot fires around the Cabana," Hawker continues. "We protected the couch with fireproof cloth, but a real smolder got started in it. The more the guys tried to put out the fire, the more oxygen got into the couch, and we had a little flare-up. Next thing you know, guys were running out the door with the smoking, burning couch. It was nothing really dangerous, but just a little crazy."

Alfred Molina was highly amused, rather than frightened, by fire that literally emanates from his hands. "Yes, I had to set fire to my fingertips," he admits with a look of utter nonchalance. "It all came

FROM FAR LEFT TO OPPOSITE: Alfred Molina is swiftly ratcheted up to the ceiling of the Arcana Cabana, performing his own stunt for this spectacular shot.

68

down to this gloopy, plasticlike stuff they put on my fingers, covered with a fire-resistant fabric. Then they put another layer of the gloopy stuff, and another layer of cloth, which they painted to look like my real hand. There was so much stuff on my fingers that they looked like four big bratwursts. Then they lit them on fire, and it gets about a minute before I started to really feel it burn, and at that point, I simply blow them out like birthday candles.

"The technology for the effect is as old as films themselves," continues Molina, "but it looks great.

We could have done it with computer graphics, but it wouldn't have looked as good. I loved it!"

Young Jake Cherry, who plays ten-year-old Dave Stutler, also had a blast performing in the sequence. "My favorite part was when I got to destroy everything with the Grimhold," he says enthusiastically. "That, to me, is awesome. My favorite thing to destroy was this really big glass case, taller than me. I pushed the Grimhold in, then jammed it out, then hit some boxes, which went flying around. I couldn't believe they were actually *letting* me break things on set!

"I also saw an early example of the visual effect when the dragon ring walks onto Dave's finger and wraps itself around him," Jake adds. "It looks so cool!"

But would Jake want a ring like that for real? "Naw," he responds immediately. "That would be creepy!"

Creepy or not, young Jake, like young Dave, discovered that if the ring fits, wear it! And for the rest of the cast and crew involved in the Arcana Cabana sequence, there was no doubt the ring fit.

THIS PAGE & OPPOSITE: Balthazar explains to an astonished and frightened 10-year-old Dave Stutler (Jake Cherry) that he's going to be great sorcerer one day; once free, Horvath struggles against Balthazar to gain control of the Grimhold, in which Horvath's cohorts are still trapped; mayhem in the Arcana Cabana ensues.

The *Enchanted* Encantus

"The people who ultimately had the responsibility for compiling the Encantus were a group led by Joan Winters, who's a graphic designer," explains Shohan. "They found a library that is part of Yale University in New Haven, Connecticut, where they were able to copy actual alchemical texts. One of Joan's people was schooled in the medieval art of bookbinding, and she did all of the aging . . . she sanded the papers, wetted them with tea, and tore them delicately so that every single page has been treated. It was enormously labor intensive, and took months to create. It has an atmosphere very close to reality, and not like some artificial prop, as if it's lived and breathed for generations."

The Encantus, the magical book of spells which Balthazar Blake gives to his apprentice, Dave Stutler, the way a high school teacher would assign *The Catcher in the Rye* to a student, is a wonderful example of the meticulous artistry of the behind-the-scenes movie talent. "In my view, it's a book not only of spells, but also an entire history of humankind's attempt to dictate natural phenomenon," says production designer Naomi Shohan. "The idea was to cover a smattering of many cultures and do it chronologically."

Helping to create, and then maintain, the Encantus was propmaster James (Jimmy) Mazzola, something of a New York movie legend himself. Mazzola's career stretches back to his first assignment, *Saturday Night Fever*, more than thirty years ago, and along the way has included dozens of landmark Big Apple shoots, including nearly twenty films directed by Woody Allen. "The Encantus is not a prop," states Mazzola. "It's fifteen hundred hand-done, hand-aged, hand-painted pages of alchemy from ancient times until the present, and it looks and feels totally real. We have different parchments from different periods of time, silk, vellum, you name it."

The "hero" version of the Encantus weighed in at a mighty seventy-five pounds—not the kind of book you want to drop on your foot—but Mazzola also fabricated a ten-pound duplicate that could be carried around when the book is closed. He even crafted a waterproofed floating version for the *Fantasia* sequence, when the underground lab becomes flooded. Aware of its import, Mazzola kept the real Encantus under lock and key in a specially created black case, just slightly less protected than the black box that always follows the president of the United States—in case of national emergencies.

TOP LEFT: Illustration for the ornate Encantus cover by Gregory Hill. LEFT, ABOVE & OPPOSITE: Pages from the Encantus, as studied by Balthazar.

BOOK
ENCANTVS

Wolves and Eagles

THE SCENE: Ten years after their initial encounter in the Arcana Cabana, it's an unwelcome reunion for NYU physics major Dave Stutler when Maxim Horvath suddenly reenters his life. Horvath is searching for the Grimhold, which the younger incarnation of Dave promptly dispensed with after exiting the Arcana Cabana all those years ago. Horvath awaits Dave's arrival in the shabby little Brooklyn apartment that he shares with roommate Bennett (Omar Benson Miller) and a lovable but slobbering bulldog named Tank. A flat consistently rattled by the elevated subway trains passing very nearby, it is, nevertheless, home. Horvath shocks the young student with his presence and threatens him with evisceration, or worse. Dave, understandably, freaks out and bolts, only to be pursued by a pack of ferocious wolves conjured up by Horvath from the pages of a monthly wildlife calendar. They chase Dave out of the apartment, up to the tracks of the elevated subway station, and are about to pounce . . . when they're suddenly transformed into adorable, face-licking puppies and a steel wing slams into the pursuing Horvath.

Dave's rescuer? It's Balthazar Blake, on a most unusual means of New York transportation: riding, like a cowboy, one of the gleaming metal Chrysler Building eagle gargoyles, which he has magically brought to life. Balthazar quickly throws a temporal displacement spell at Horvath, seriously impeding his ability to pursue, and takes off into the night skies with Dave as a terrified, but relieved, passenger.

BEHIND THE SCENE: "When we said that we wanted to bring New York to life for the movie," says

ABOVE: One of the beautiful—and remarkably friendly—wolves on set at Steiner Studios. OPPOSITE: The wondrous computer-controlled Chrysler eagle in the cavernous interior of the Bedford Armory in Brooklyn, where major portions of the film were shot.

Jerry Bruckheimer, "we meant that quite literally." Adds Jon Turteltaub, "We looked for places to find sorcery and magic in Manhattan. If you're ever there and looking at the Chrysler Building—which is a magical structure in itself—and you look up, there are these extraordinarily beautiful steel-and-aluminum eagles that are used as gargoyles. We saw those guys and said, 'that's in the movie.'"

Although the wolf chase and eagle rescue plays out for a relatively brief amount of screen time, it required one studio set, one large exterior set, a real "practical" location, four actual wolves, one huge mechanical Chrysler eagle, and another complex digital version of the same. The first beat of the scene was filmed inside of Dave's apartment set at Steiner Studios on the very first day of principal photography. The next beat was shot on day seventy-three in the Marcy Avenue elevated subway station in Williamsburg,

Brooklyn. And finally, the sequence was completed on days seventy-eight and seventy-nine in a full-size reproduction of the Marcy Avenue station constructed at Floyd Bennett Field in Brooklyn. The work wasn't limited to on-set activity. To do the real Marcy Avenue station in Brooklyn (as opposed to the "reel" one re-created at Bennett Field), crew members were obliged to take a six-hour MTA track safety class offered by the Metropolitan Transit Authority, which operates most public transportation in New York City. That's dedication—and showbiz.

As much a part of the scene as the sets, the four handsome wolves, under the supervision of the film's animal wrangler, Steve McAuliff, and trained by Jill Marie Chambers and Robin Seremba, go by the names of Bandit, Sierra, Samson, and Takoda. They reside at Mike Hodanish's Hallingwoods Farm, a rescue service center in Jackson, New Jersey. "Even though the wolves in the movie are portrayed as being ferocious, these animals are actually very friendly," notes Hodanish. He's not wrong. Upon approaching the majestic creatures, one is amazed by their gentleness. "They're very social, they love attention, and they love people," Hodanish adds.

"I had to audition real wolves, how crazy is that?" asks Jon Turteltaub, laughing. "You know what it's like to tell a wolf, 'I'm sorry, but no, thank you'? My goodness, are they beautiful animals. They're everything you'd expect from a dog, except the part when they get a little upset and you notice that the wolf has your esophagus in its mouth. Then you start thinking, 'OK, I'd better change my direction, be a little nicer.'"

In fact, the four wolves were almost too nice, and their distinct lack of primal bloodlust made for some trying times as the trainers attempted to literally get them up to speed while chasing Jay Baruchel around the set. It is probably safe to say, however, that was fine with the human cast, most specifically Baruchel.

The Chrysler eagle came in two varieties, the practical, motion-base version constructed by multiple Academy Award–winning special-effects coordinator John Frazier, and one that would be created later via CG by visual-effects supervisor John Nelson and the artists at Asylum Visual Effects (which was splitting the VFX work between themselves and Double Negative Visual Effects of London).

"We first built a quarter-scale working model of the Chrysler eagle together in our Los Angeles facility," says Frazier, "and once that was approved we faced the challenge of building a full-size, computer-controlled version on a motion base. We built the eagle in Los Angeles and shipped it to New York,

and then special-effects foreman Mark Hawker and his team controlled and operated the six-axle motion base."

"You can't really beat it for movement," explains Hawker, "and it's something that can be set up relatively quick. High precision, all motion control, run off a computer. It has six degrees of movement, and a little bit of rotation. It has a lot of hydraulics, motion controlled with a little joystick, and that's what we manipulate to get all the movements we want. But we can also record the movements so that it does exactly the same thing on every take."

Performing on the Chrysler eagle motion base certainly gave Jay Baruchel some thrills. "When you're acting on a fifty-foot-tall iron eagle head it's kind of hard not to be like a little kid. It's like being on the coolest amusement park ride in the world."

It was production designer Naomi Shohan who designed the Chrysler eagle as it comes to life on the big screen. Retaining the brilliance of architect William

Van Alen's original 1928 Art Deco genius (the actual eagle gargoyles on the building were modeled to resemble hood ornaments of the Chrysler Plymouth as it appeared in the late 1920s), Shohan also gave it a little tweak here and there. "We changed the eagle's beak and eyes to make them a little more sinister, but otherwise we were quite faithful."

And so, in the spirit of the entire movie, Naomi Shohan kept what made the original so special, and then added a new and unique twist. "We wanted to respect the past," notes Jerry Bruckheimer, "without becoming enslaved by it. We were free to make these magical elements truly live by infusing them with something new."

ABOVE: Tani Kunitake's beautiful illustration of the Chrysler eagle soaring high over Manhattan. OPPOSITE: The great metal Art Deco eagle swoops down from its usual perch on the parapet of the Chrysler Building, as brought to life by VFX-supervisor John Nelson and Asylum Visual Effects.

The Most *Unforgettable* Chinese Festival

THE SCENE: Balthazar and Dave's mission to find the Grimhold Dave "misplaced" years ago takes them to an old acupuncturist shop in Chinatown. The shop is attended by an old woman who's seemingly innocuous . . . until she transforms into Horvath, who releases ancient sorcerer Sun Lok (Gregory Woo) from the Grimhold. A furious fight inside the shop soon spills outside, where a raucous Chinese celebration is taking place, with dancers, drummers, and brightly colored confetti. As bystanders look on in confused horror, Sun Lok transforms a parade dragon manned by festival dancers into a terrifyingly real creature, which proceeds to chase Dave through a building and onto a fire escape high above the frenetic scene below.

BEHIND THE SCENE: With New York as much a central character in the story of *The Sorcerer's Apprentice* as the sorcerers themselves, it only made sense to take full advantage of the city's Chinatown in Lower Manhattan. It is, without a doubt, one of the most vibrant, colorful, and exciting communities in the United States. "You want to talk about magic," states director Jon Turteltaub, "go to New York's Chinatown. Most cities have a Chinatown that's a block long, but

the Chinatown in New York has a population that's probably more than that of a lot of cities in the United States. It's an amazingly cool place."

"We were determined to film major sequences in some of the most famous neighborhoods of New York," says Jerry Bruckheimer, "no matter how challenging. And Chinatown is incredibly challenging, because it's a thriving community filled with commerce and people going about their business. What we wanted to do was make them an integral part of the shoot. In fact, we couldn't possibly have filmed the sequence without the cooperation and participation of the people living and working in the area."

Selected as the site of the major sequence of magic and action was Eldridge Street, between Canal and Division streets, in the heart of Chinatown. On March 7, 2009, an open call for the epic sequence was organized at the 109-year-old Lin Sing Association, the largest such community-assistance group in Chinatown, in the historic district on Mott Street. Senior casting associate Grant Wilfley expected, perhaps, eight hundred people to show up for the five hundred available background players required. "We posted in two of the Chinese newspapers and on a local Chinese-language television station. But I guess the Disney and Bruckheimer names were magic, because more than two thousand people showed up."

The queue snaked its way outside the small entrance on Mott, around the corner, and all the way up Bayard Street, twisting up Mulberry as well. Ranging from teens to octogenarians, it was near pandemonium, but everyone managed to keep their cool and good humor. "The problem for us was dealing with the language barrier," confesses Wilfley, but several people from the community were there

to assist, including Eddie Chiu, who heads the Lin Sing Association and is one of the best-known community leaders in Chinatown. "I never expected so many people," Chiu admits, surrounded by hordes of aspiring background players, some of them spectacularly clad in traditional Chinese costumes. "The first ones lined up at six a.m. [in the] morning and our casting didn't start until ten. But I'm glad, because we need more tourism coming to Chinatown, and *The Sorcerer's Apprentice* will highlight how fascinating this neighborhood really is."

The Sorcerer's Apprentice company took over Eldridge Street for two solid weeks of all-night filming. This extraordinarily atmospheric street, framed by the Manhattan Bridge and the noisy subway trains careening back and forth from Manhattan to Brooklyn, is primarily populated by Fukienese Chinese from Fujian Province, having migrated into the neighborhood some fifteen years earlier and replacing earlier waves

TOP: The seemingly harmless parade dragon before it is brought to life by sorcerer Sun Lok. ABOVE: Balthazar holding the Grimhold.

ABOVE: Members of New York's Chinese community eagerly participate in the festival sequence filmed on Eldridge Street.
BELOW RIGHT: Jay Baruchel and Jerry Bruckheimer chat during a long night's work in Chinatown.

of immigrants from Eastern Europe (mainly Jews; the historic Eldridge Street Synagogue still maintains a congregation as well as a museum) and Puerto Rico. Eldridge Street is famous to New York foodies for restaurants specializing in Lanzhou-style hand-pulled noodles, their simplicity, Formica tabletops, and plastic bowls belying the gourmet quality of their fare. Many a crew member ducked into these restaurants to get a steaming-hot bowl of soup, dumplings, and noodles to fortify them during the long nights of filming in the often chilly March air.

"The true, unsung heroes on a movie like this are the location managers," says director Jon Turteltaub during a three a.m. break in filming. "Securing contracts from every person on Eldridge Street, asking some stores to close, others to stay open, putting lights on their buildings, putting confetti on their rooftops, making it all safe. Then you have the specialty people from the community, like the dancers inside the parade dragon, the tai chi fan dancers, the drummers; and on top of that, you have stunts, fire effects, rickety fire escapes, subway trains going by.

"You can't do a scene like this on the back lot," continues Turteltaub. "And I think all of the people who were participating in the parade and as background were having fun. Once the music and drumming starts it gets exciting. The dragon and confetti are exciting. And then it gets really exciting when Nic Cage comes out to set. There's just a really good atmosphere. It may sound corny, but when you're making a Disney movie, people know that it's going to have some warmth to it, that it's going to feel good. This scene, although action-packed, is a celebration of New York Chinatown, which makes people feel better on set."

"It took us five months of planning to get us to close Eldridge Street to traffic for two weeks," says executive producer Barry Waldman, a veteran of several hugely scaled Jerry Bruckheimer films, among them the *National Treasure* duo, *Armageddon*, and *Pearl Harbor*. "Every business on the street had to agree to allow us to film here. We were fortunate that during the planning stages they had the sixty-seventh annual Fukienese New Year celebration, and we were invited. We paid for a table, came in, ate with them, showed a lot of respect, and welcomed their New Year. They immediately embraced us as a company that wasn't coming in like an invading army.

"We've tried to be very respectful," Waldman continues, "reducing the amount of noise as the night goes on, and when we leave in the morning, the street is open for business. The payoff is that when you shoot on a back lot, you have to create Chinatown. When you shoot on Eldridge Street, you're *in* Chinatown, the flavor, feeling, and community are already there."

Halfway through the week's shoot on Eldridge Street, Jay Baruchel was like a kid in the proverbial candy shop. Twelve air movers mounted on the roofs of Eldridge Street buildings blew three thousand pounds of multicolored confetti everywhere, adding more visual backdrop to the already brilliantly decorated street. Production designer Naomi Shohan and her team added some twenty illuminated light-box signs and colorful red lanterns strung from one end of the street to the other. "Look at this," Baruchel says, looking around him with wide eyes. "I think there are five billion people on this street right now. And confetti is infinitely nicer than snow; as someone who lives in Montreal, I can attest to that. This scene is an amazing testament to how authentic the visuals in this movie are. We've been shooting in so many iconic New York places, and I just hope that we haven't annoyed too many people who live in this neighborhood. They've been real kind, and many of them seem psyched to have us here."

Indeed, some nights took on the air of a cheerful block party, with neighborhood residents enjoying the unusual spectacle. "It's impossible not to fall in love with the work when there's this much energy and this much going on," Baruchel adds. "It informs your performance, and you have a lot to react to."

Gregory Woo portrays ancient Chinese sorcerer Sun Lok, released from the Grimhold by Horvath.

breakaway walls we've ever done, and we had wall-rippers giving the illusion of the dragon smashing through the hallway. Then the dragon gets stuck and blasts a big fireball, which were propane cannons that we installed inside of the set. So we did the destruction elements and fireballs, but John Nelson and his visual-effects team created the dragon itself."

"Chinatown was a very big deal," acknowledges Nelson, "with multiple levels of visual effects on a grand scale. People fighting, things morphing, things exploding, and, of course, Sun Lok bringing the dragon to life, and then Balthazar casting a confetti spell."

"How do the sorcerers who don't want the world to know there's really magic cover it up so that the crowds of people in the festival don't know that it's a real dragon?" asks Turteltaub. It is a question he had fun answering. "It gets really complicated, [especially as] the only way to destroy the dragon is to destroy the sorcerer who is controlling the dragon, which is one of the lessons that Dave has to quickly learn."

Creating a believable digital dragon took a bit of magic, too. It was, in fact, one of the biggest challenges of all faced by Nelson and the team from Asylum Visual Effects. "The dragon is as big as a truck," he notes, "and if something like that were really on that Chinatown street, it would be generating a lot of follow-through. We do primary animation for the character, and then secondary animation for its muscles, and then what we call effects animation for what the dragon would generate, whether steam, spray, confetti, or dirt. All of those things work together to make the illusions seem real. We tried to make it all work in conjunction with the performances of the actors, and the magic that *they* generate."

The result is a truly stunning visual display that will have even the most jaded of New Yorkers looking at the city—and especially Chinatown—in a whole new, magical way.

81

Portraying sorcerer Sun Lok was a cultural revelation to actor Gregory Woo, a handsome young all-American boy who just happens to also be Chinese, and whose startling physical transformation frightened at least a few small children watching the Chinatown filming. "I grew up in a small town, Round Rock, Texas," he confesses, "and moved to New York to study acting. Every day I would ride my bicycle over the Manhattan Bridge overlooking Eldridge Street, and never knew that I would be standing here in this huge set, with the beautiful parade dragon and so many amazing people. Growing up, I just wanted to be like any other kid in Round Rock, but my parents instilled in me that it was OK to look different.

"Look at me now," Woo laughs, showing off his bald-pated, pointy-eared, animal-eyed, long-finger-nailed Sun Lok look. "This is as different as it gets."

And although special-effects foreman Mark Hawker blew fireballs out of an actual Eldridge Street apartment building, the more destructive elements of the scene were reserved for sets constructed inside the Bedford Armory; a nearly full-size, exact duplicate of the facade of the building where Dave Stutler tries to escape from the dragon, as well as the interior of a beauty salon utterly destroyed by the creature as it chases its prey. "We had twelve ratchets busting all the breakaway glass and pulling the furniture," explains Hawker. "They were the biggest, thickest

THIS PAGE: Early concept illustrations by Dean Tschetter of Sun Lok's emergence from the Grimhold, a scene which was substantially altered in the final film. OPPOSITE: Gregory Woo embraces the character of Sun Lok.
PAGES 84–85: Tani Kunitake's epic conceptual illustration of the parade dragon coming to life and creating havoc during the Chinatown festival.

A Love Letter to *Tesla*

As Nicolas Cage pointed out during his farewell to the assembled *Sorcerer's Apprentice* company on the last day of filming, Friday, July 11, 2009, "For those of you who don't believe in magic, today is Nikola Tesla's birthday."

To be exact, it was the 153rd birthday of the great Tesla. The controversial and brilliant inventor's revolutionary theories and spiritual endeavors constantly challenged the scientific and business establishments of his day—and continue to amaze and baffle more than a century later.

"We all love Nikola Tesla," states Jerry Bruckheimer. "I think he was a genius, and unfortunately, he never got the credit that he deserved while he was alive."

"This movie is definitely a love letter to Tesla," says Jay Baruchel. "He spent his life essentially working on scientifically created magic. Magic *is* science. And science has proven that humans are just vibrating energy."

Nikola Tesla, an ethnic Serb who was born in what is now Croatia and was then an Austrian province, emigrated to the United States in 1884. He's the father of alternating current (AC) power systems, which helped bring forth the Second Industrial Revolution, and pioneered modern electrical engineering. Among his résumé qualifications, Tesla worked for Thomas Edison, who promised the twenty-eight-year-old a hefty sum to redesign motors and generators, but ended up paying him a mere eighteen dollars per week.

Tesla and Edison would become rivals during their "War of the Currents," with the latter favoring direct current (DC) for electrical

Nikola Tesla (1856–1943)

power distribution, although it couldn't be transmitted more than a mile, over Tesla's much more efficient AC, which could radiate outward for hundreds of miles. Another rival of Edison's, George Westinghouse, went into alliance with Tesla. In 1893, their AC system illuminated the

Chicago World's Fair, and in 1895, transformed Niagara Falls into a producer of mass amounts of electricity with the first hydroelectric power plant.

The list of Tesla's inventions is beyond staggering, with seven hundred worldwide patents to his credit. He discovered that high-frequency alternating current, transformed by a device now known as a "Tesla coil," could send signals through the air invisibly and without wires. He invented, among many things, modern radio, although Guglielmo Marconi took both the credit and the patent (overturned by the U.S. Supreme Court in 1943 to favor Tesla), fluorescent lighting, laser beams, remote control, the Tesla induction motor, and an electric car. But despite these triumphs, financial fortune ultimately eluded Tesla. He was, instead, increasingly perceived as eccentric at best, a mad scientist at worst. A man obsessed with pigeons, Tesla spent the last ten years of his life in room 3327 of the New Yorker Hotel in Manhattan, destitute and riddled with debts. He died on January 7, 1943.

Screenwriter Matt Lopez decided to bring Nikola Tesla into *The Sorcerer's Apprentice* script during his research for the film. "There was a Tesla biography written several years ago that referred to him as 'a modern sorcerer,' which I thought was curious. I started reading more and more about Tesla and discovered that many contemporary newspaper accounts of his time also called him a sorcerer. I went further into this idea of the link between science and the realm of the fantastic that's always existed, but known to a select few." Thus, in the film,

Illustration by Dean Tschetter of the Tesla coils radiating energy in Dave's underground training room.

Balthazar Blake is delighted to discover that Dave has been experimenting with Tesla coils. "All these years you thought you were running away from sorcery," he tells the younger man. "It's not a coincidence you built these electrical field generators, Dave. This is your magic. Dr. Tesla was my friend and a great Merlinean."

In fact, during his own research for the film, Nicolas Cage actually decided to stay for a night in the exact room at the New Yorker where Tesla spent his last decade. "Nic stayed there to kind of channel some of that energy, and thought it was a really interesting experience," notes executive producer Mike Stenson. "Tesla invented things that certainly would have been considered sorcery or magic to people in earlier centuries, like radio and technology, transmitting energy through the air. We're still catching up to him today."

There are numerous direct mentions and allusions to Nikola Tesla throughout the film, including an important scene of dialogue between Balthazar and Dave on the parapet of the Chrysler Building in which the older sorcerer carefully handles a pigeon, subtly honoring the bird-loving scientist.

What's more, director of photography Bojan Bazelli, something of a sorcerer himself with a camera who, like Tesla, is Serbian, enjoyed pointing out that he attended a high school in what was then known as Yugoslavia, named after the great inventor. The nods continued. The company shot on a location that happened to be a stone's throw from Nikola Tesla Way. And just down the street from an apartment building where a good many of the film's out-of-town crew stayed during production was the Serbian Orthodox Church on 25th Street in Chelsea. Just to the left of the church's entrance was a bust of, yes, Nikola Tesla. And the company filmed at the Cathedral of St. John the Divine on 110th Street, where Tesla received a state funeral attended by more than two thousand people.

Coincidence or magic?

At this point, do you even have to ask?

Sorcerer *in Training*

THE SCENE: Inside a huge old underground subway turnaround, which Dave Stutler uses as his laboratory, Balthazar Blake proceeds to teach—or rather, *tries* to teach—his apprentice the art of sorcery with the help of the Encantus. Much trial and error ensues as Dave learns not only to control his powers, but also the meaning behind those powers. To do so, he must also learn to let go of his preconceived notions of what is *science* and what is *magic*.

BEHIND THE SCENE: A sequence composed of individual beats both thrilling and comical, Dave's sorcerer-training scenes demanded the full talents not only of Nicolas Cage and Jay Baruchel, but also Jon Turteltaub and Jerry Bruckheimer's entire team of behind-the-scenes artists. "Jon wants to keep the magic in the film as true as possible," notes Bruckheimer, "so as much as possible is done in front of the camera. And in keeping with [that] important aspect of the film, we're trying to take the physics and magic, and make them work together in a believable way. The idea is that sorcery and magic are not mutually exclusive, which is the most important lesson that Dave has to learn from Balthazar."

"Being a sorcerer is a mixture of your own innate ability, your ability to learn and to study, and certain physical qualities that you were born with," explains Jon Turteltaub. "Some may call that talent. You know, Wayne Gretzky didn't just learn how to become a great hockey player, there was something about Wayne Gretzky that just made him good at it. Same with an artist, a singer, or a sorcerer. You're born with

ABOVE: Balthazar and apprentice Dave stand in the forbidden domain of the Merlin Circle; OPPOSITE: Illustration of sorcerer training in the underground lab, by Dean Tschetter.

that power, and once you have it, then you need to learn how to master it. However, sorcery and science aren't separate. A transducer is any mechanism that transfers one form of energy into another form of energy. For example, an antenna gets some electronic vibrations, turns them into waves, and then it goes to your television. Sorcerers either have a ring, like Balthazar and Dave, or maybe the tip of a cane, like Horvath.

"It was really important to me that this film be about embracing science in magic," continues Turteltaub. "To me, all the magic in the world is in science. That's where all the wonder comes from. And science is under attack by people who are afraid of losing a sense of wonder in the world. But the people

who wonder more than anyone are the scientists. They dream these things, then look for ways to make it happen. The essence of Dave as a physicist is a reflection of that innate talent he has as a sorcerer, that has drawn him toward wanting to see how the mysteries of life work, but also give him the knowledge to be able to learn much quicker.

"So Dave has to go through a rigorous training program," Turteltaub goes on. "Balthazar has to put Dave through all the paces that challenge him psychologically, as well as train him, and it's not going to be without pain. [Dave] needs to learn how to focus his mental energies, he's got to learn how to create energy and matter and use them as defensive weapons. How not to get hit in the face. How to transform one piece of matter into another. And he's doing all of this in his lab that was previously used just for science experiments for school, which now becomes Dave's proving ground."

And a proving ground it most certainly is. To help Dave in his training, Balthazar has a plethora of techniques—and he doesn't hesitate to use the various spells and abilities. "The big gun, as I call it," says Nicolas Cage, "is the plasma bolt. When you're really in trouble, you can generate all of this power and shoot it out of your hand in a bolt of electricity." He pauses before adding, "Just as important as the spells are the ethics of being a Merlinean: the stronger the man, the stronger the source, you have to not use shortcuts, you have to be responsible with the power, you can't just play with it like it's a toy for personal

89

gain." This is a lesson Dave will learn all too quickly. A lesson, in fact, he's been learning since the day he went into the Arcana Cabana.

Stunt coordinator George Marshall Ruge worked carefully with Cage and Baruchel to ensure maximum excitement for the audience and minimal damage to the actors, although the rigors of what they needed to accomplish meant that every day of the sorcerer-training sequence was a full-body workout. "Shooting the training scenes was real fun, and murder on my body," admits Jay Baruchel. "The most physical thing that I do on average when I'm not working is getting up to go to the bathroom during TV commercial breaks. So to go from that to saving the world is daunting if nothing else. In the training sequences, I get to throw myself all over the room and flail like crazy."

Jay Baruchel, however, is blessed with the kind of body that is as capable of expression as his remarkably flexible and fluid face, and which the young actor uses with the exquisite control of a premier danseur. The more out of control Dave seems to be, the more in control Jay Baruchel is. It's a beautiful deception. "Physical comedy is the reason I got into acting, you know," confesses Baruchel. "Rowan Atkinson is my absolute hero. I've seen every *Mr. Bean* episode ever made. So anytime I get the chance to be remotely

physical, I inject it into every job I do, much to the chagrin of whoever's hired me. I've been tripping and falling down on purpose my whole life, so I figured that I might as well find a way to get paid for it. If it's funny, physical comedy is the purest form because it requires no translation. There's nothing left to the subtlety or nuances of the language. Regardless of what language you speak, what religion you practice, or where you live, everybody finds someone falling down and getting their butt kicked funny."

"I very rarely have laughed out loud on set," confesses executive producer Mike Stenson of Jerry Bruckheimer Films, "but that's what happened to me while I was watching Jay in this scene. There's a moment when he's in the middle of his training, and he's trying to block lightning bolts coming off the Tesla coils, but not very successfully. It's like he's being shocked with giant Tasers over and over again, and what Jay does with that in terms of his body movements and range as a physical comedian is really great."

"The training room scenes are pretty mind-blowing," says Baruchel. "There's something called the Merlin Circle, which has seven domains for different elements of life and human existence. There's a scene where Balthazar conjures it up in the underground lab, and all of a sudden, this gorgeous, ancient-looking carving in the middle of the floor comes to life in fires of different colors, green, red, yellow. It's impossible not to be affected by that when you're standing right beside it. It really informs your performance. It also really affects your performance, 'cause it's hot as hell and I was constantly worried that it was gonna set my shoes on fire. When you see all of the scenes with me and fire in this movie, you can rest assured that all I was thinking about was, 'Please, this is not how I care to go, I have more stuff I wanna to do in my life.'" At one point, after one of the pyrotechnic effects, a somewhat rattled Baruchel apologized to a

crew member for not answering a question by saying, "Sorry, but the fire hijacked my imagination."

It actually took a lot of imagination to create the fire within the Merlin Circle. Asks Jon Turteltaub, "Did you know that there is some fire that's hotter than other fire? Did you know that there is fire that comes in different colors? Just sit on set and watch as a special-effects guy pours a special liquid, lights it on fire, and the actor goes, 'Why am I standing in that, can't you do this later?' But you can't. So you get the costume people, and they make fireproof costumes, so that when Nic Cage is standing in the middle of the fire, he's not *on* fire. And that means that you're being saved $50,000 in visual effects later on, because you're using real life, which looks cool when you're shooting it. That's what's special about special effects. The actors aren't pretending to be standing in fire, they're *really* standing in fire. It makes the performances better, which obviously makes the movie better."

"One of the reasons I had such a long prep on the show was because so many of the effects had to be built into the underground lab set while it was being built instead of coming in afterward," notes Mark Hawker. "The Merlin Circle fire was, of course, one of those. We placed the fire rods six inches below the deck in a water tank, sort of like a gigantic stovetop burner, and then built a water cooling system into the fire. Steel troughs were built into the floor, and the set was constructed around that. We had two different systems for the Merlin Circle. The initial one was for the scene in which Balthazar first burned it into the stone floor. Jon Turteltaub didn't want to use regular flames, but for it to have a different life to it. Then, for the training sequences, we'd light up certain symbols in the Merlin Circle, surface burns that were either red,

blue, or purple. We used something called Panther felt, which holds lamp oil and burns for a long time."

For the training sequences, Nicolas Cage and Jay Baruchel got their chance to literally hold fire in their hands. "We rigged them with little hoses that came up their arms, with a copper coil in their hands with Panther felt," explains Hawker. "Then we apply a gel to protect them from feeling the heat. You just light it up and let it burn. At some point, we snuff out the fire, and then John Nelson's visual effects will make that fire jump out of their hands and fly across the room."

Another nifty trick devised by the filmmakers was a device that created a practical light source for scenes in which the sorcerers are compressing plasma in their hands. "We worked with our chief lighting technician, Tony Nakonechnyj, and gaffer Michael Gallart on this," Nelson explains, "which allows the camera to see the plasma actually growing in the hands of the actors. It casts a beautiful interactive light." Although the device was practical, with an LED light and wires, Nelson would replace that in the computers later, creating CG plasma but retaining the real glow emitted by the wonderful little gizmo.

Also helping to create magic was director of photography Bojan Bazelli; Nakonechnyj and Gallart; key grip Tom Prate; and their extensive and very hardworking crews, who created a huge and sophisticated lighting grid inside the underground lab set for the sorcerer-training sequences. "We had the biggest available 'space light,'" notes Bazelli, "which could be raised and lowered. But that was only providing an ambience illumination. The three lighting grids around it provided computerized, interactive lighting. That provided bursts of light, which gave you

ABOVE: Special-effects coordinator Mark Hawker holds flame in his hand, using a specially created device. BELOW LEFT: Director Jon Turteltaub watches as special-effects supervisor John Frazier and coordinator Hawker's crew prepare the Merlin Circle to ignite.

the feeling that they were traveling through space, like the plasma bolts being thrown by Balthazar and Dave."

Jon Turteltaub, who had engaged Bazelli for the film after the cinematographer was strongly recommended by Jerry Bruckheimer, soon understood why he had impressed the megaproducer so much. "I had ideas for what I wanted *The Sorcerer's Apprentice* to look like," confesses the director, "but Bojan Bazelli showed me what it *should* look like. He shot this movie in a way different than anything I've done before. Nobody on a movie works completely on their own and does things unilaterally. Everything is a collaboration. And after seeing what Bojan was pushing me to do, I fell in love with it. Bojan shoots with wide lenses, which really puts the characters within a huge space and can get you some very dramatic looks. They're dynamic, and make the frame full.

"That allowed us to see more of the magic," Turteltaub goes on. "Lets things seem grander, and gave the movie a kind of Gothic, romantic style, where things look a little bit larger than life."

Which is, after all, what movies are supposed to be all about.

91

THIS PAGE: Balthazar trains a sometimes reluctant Dave in the underground lab. OPPOSITE: Dean Tschetter's illustration of Dave being hit by a Tesla coil's blast.

The *Merlin* Circle

From the floor of Dave's lab to the sky above New York City, the Merlin Circle is one of the omnipresent symbols of *The Sorcerer's Apprentice*. And that is not without reason. When the film was first conceived, it was important to all that a connection was made with not only the original poem and film inspirations, but also with the legend of sorcery itself. Out of this was born the Merlin Circle as seen in the film.

Much research went into crafting this unique circle. The seven domains as created and envisioned by Naomi Shohan represent Space-Time, Motion, Matter, Elements, Transformation, and Mind. At the center of it all lies the Forbidden Domain/Love. It is this domain that Dave must learn to control if he is to ever become the true Prime Merlinian. It is also, as Balthazar explains, the reason for Morgana's betrayal. "The Forbidden Domain," he tells Dave. "Power over life and death itself. Merlin was the only one who could access its power. Morgana wanted to learn its secrets, but Merlin refused. So she killed him."

The history of alchemy and the circles that symbolize it is not without some negative connotations. Some associate it with witchcraft and evil, but that is not its original intent—nor the intent of the one in the movie. The circle is a symbol that dates back in various forms to ancient China and to Egypt as far back as

ABOVE: The Merlin Circle.
OPPOSITE: Balthazar Blake, Sorcerer of the 777th degree, brings the Merlin Circle to fiery and powerful life in this image from Double Negative Visual Effects.

1900 BC, and made its way into the European conscience by the thirteenth century. While the specifics have changed and evolved with the time and place, it has most often been a symbol of unity and spirituality, a guide.

For *The Sorcerer's Apprentice*, this is especially true. The Merlin Circle is a source of true good. Something that if mistreated or abused can do great harm. However, the true and absolute strength it holds—the Forbidden Domain—can only be accessed by great sacrifice and a pure heart.

In the case of this circle, the true import is in the naming and history of it. Jon Turteltaub recognized the power of the Arthurian tradition. "You want to ground even a fantasy in something the audience understands," he notes, "and you can have a shorthand. When you say the name 'Merlin,' everyone gets it. There's a nobility, a sense of honor, and quest for goodness. When you say the name 'Morgana,' it's the opposite of all those things, the seven deadly sins in one person." Setting the story in the context of Arthurian mythology gives the film a greater scope, because the audience understands the grand context of it all.

"It also doesn't hurt that Disney, with *The Sword and the Stone*, has its own history with Arthurian legends," notes the director. "In our film, the special dragon ring that Balthazar is trying to give to whoever the special apprentice is really is made up of the metal from the sword, Excalibur, and the stone it was pulled from. So in a sense, that ring is the new sword and the stone."

College *Bathrooms* and Quicksand *Rugs*

THE SCENES: Two exciting scenes; two examples of sorcery in action. The first of those scenes finds Dave cornered by Maxim Horvath and Drake Stone (Toby Kebbell) in a New York University men's room, and rescued thanks to the welcome intervention of Balthazar Blake. The second occurs when Balthazar and Horvath duke it out in Drake Stone's preposterously lavish penthouse in a sorcerer-style throwdown.

BEHIND THE SCENES: Having performed stellar work on two of the biggest and most successful movie trilogies of all time—Peter Jackson's *The Lord of the Rings* and Jerry Bruckheimer and Gore Verbinski's *Pirates of the Caribbean*—as well as on Bruckheimer and Jon Turteltaub's two action-packed *National Treasure* films, George Marshall Ruge was the obvious choice as stunt coordinator for *The Sorcerer's Apprentice*. "George is one of those stunt coordinators who really thinks about the story and doesn't want the stunts to overshadow it," says executive producer Barry Waldman. "It's a real key component of why George is always invited to the party. He's one of those guys who comes from a real filmmaker background, versus 'I can make it bigger, better, badder.' It's not what George and his guys are about. They're really smart, and really subtle."

"I was excited, because I grew up with *Fantasia* in my memory bank," says Ruge, who belies the stereotype of his profession by being surprisingly soft-spoken and modest (but also intensely focused when at work). "This is my sixth film with the Bruckheimer family. Jerry is the consummate producer and always assembles [a] very eclectic and caring crew. Jon has become a friend ever since the

ABOVE: Steadicam operator films a furious fight between Balthazar and Horvath in the NYU men's room set.
BELOW: As Drake Stone, actor Toby Kebbell is hurled backward on a pulley.

first *National Treasure*. He's a great person, and a real humanitarian, which is the thing I love about his films. Jon always manages to bring out the humanity within his films, even if it involves sorcery.

"The fight involving Balthazar, Dave, Horvath, and Drake Stone in the NYU Athletic Building men's room was another mind-boggler," notes Ruge. "We have some spectacular stunt work, which is absolutely real, such as when Balthazar hurls Stone across the room and slams him off the tile wall. Audiences may think that it's CG, but not so."

"The bathroom scene was brilliant," enthuses Toby Kebbell, who portrays Drake Stone. "I got thrown backward on a big pulley system, and I think I almost lost one of my testicles in the process in that harness. Stunt players are the ones who save us all, so getting to do a little snippet of that is like being a tough guy. And when you're wearing four-inch [platform] heels and skintight pants, like I was as Drake Stone, you need to feel a little bit macho."

"That scene when I get jumped in the bathroom was just crazy," adds Jay Baruchel. "Drake Stone lifts me up and just leaves me hanging against the wall. He's incredibly *under*whelmed by Dave, who's supposed to be a powerful sorcerer but is actually a 140-pound awkward kid with a very pale complexion and funny-looking clothes. So when Horvath and Drake Stone corner me, it looks like my minutes are numbered. But then, a certain thousand-year-old sorcerer by the name of Balthazar Blake comes to my aid and basically beats the crap out of Drake Stone.

"Balthazar throws Drake into a whole bunch of

The "carpet gag," in which Balthazar sinks into a rug in Drake Stone's penthouse that has taken on the consistency of quicksand.

lockers, and that was cool to watch," recalls Baruchel with a happy smile. "It was also cool to watch someone else do the harness gag. I was like, ha-ha, enjoy yourself, Toby, good luck to you!"

A sequence from a later point in the story again pits the opposing sorcerers against each other, this time in Drake Stone's ludicrously overdecorated penthouse apartment. The scene presented challenges both for Ruge and the special-effects teams, as well as for Nicolas Cage, particularly when, as sometimes happen on movie sets, things didn't exactly go like clockwork. For a "gag" in which Horvath transforms a Persian rug in Drake's apartment into a deadly quicksand trap for Balthazar, Nicolas Cage took an accidental bath. He was standing on what amounted to a latex membrane with a hydraulic elevator

underneath, which when dropped, filled with water to give the impression that Balthazar was being funneled up to his neck in quicksand (with visual effects completing the effect in postproduction). In truth, he would be protected by the latex and be in an almost hermetically sealed bubble. But at one point, the latex broke and it became a small swimming pool.

No problem. Cage, without complaint, was dried off, the latex was replaced, and twenty minutes later they shot the scene over again. And again, until Jon Turteltaub was satisfied with the results.

Mark Hawker further explains the quicksand-rug-technique process: "Construction cut a hole in the center of the floor of the Drake Stone penthouse set, and we built a ten-foot-deep, twelve-by-twenty tank. In that tank, we have a platform that raises and

lowers, and drops about six feet. We bring that up to the surface of the water, when it's filled to the top of the floor. And, across that, is a huge sheet of latex. Nic walks out on the latex, and as he starts walking, we begin dropping the floor slowly. His feet are stepping in four inches of water with the latex, and you start getting this little wave action. We just keep sinking and sinking it as he walks, up to his knees and then his waist. When I tested the gag, it was a very strange feeling. You got all of this water pressure just pushing up against you."

And how does Hawker explain the minor mishap? "I think it was because Nic was wearing Balthazar Blake's pointy sorcerer shoes," he responds with a smile. It would seem, sometimes, even the most powerful of magic can't fix everything.

THE SCENE: A serious altercation in the underground lab between Merlineans Balthazar Blake and Dave Stutler on one side and Morganians Maxim Horvath and Drake Stone on the other ends in a car chase through the streets of New York City, in which the vehicles magically morph into other vehicles and enter a bizarre "mirror world" in which everything (except their vehicles) is in reverse. Just consider the endless possibilities. . . .

BEHIND THE SCENE: "We have huge adventures all throughout Manhattan, including a magical car chase," notes Jon Turteltaub. "It's a Jerry Bruckheimer movie, you've got to have a car chase. Are you kidding? You sign a piece of paper when you work with Jerry: 'Yes, sir, I'll do a car chase.' But how do *sorcerers* have a car chase? How do you play on that? What makes it different than a typical chase scene? Anyone can drive fast and get into accidents, but how do we do it differently? You've got to use the magic."

"We not only wanted a car chase even more exciting than the one that Jon directed in London on *National Treasure: Book of Secrets*," says Jerry Bruckheimer. "We wanted one the likes of which has never been seen on-screen before."

"Everything takes on a magical flair you would not normally anticipate from a car chase sequence," says Nicolas Cage. "Cars morph into other cars, they go into a mirror world at one point. They're operating by a whole different list of physics and rules than you would normally assume for a car chase to have."

"In prepping the sequence, we had to think, 'All right, if I were a sorcerer, how would I have a car chase?'" says Turteltaub. "Your car doesn't have to stay your car and your environment doesn't have to stay your environment. In typical car chases, your obstacles are the other cars on the road, the environment you're in, and the other person you're chasing or being chased by. But if you're a sorcerer, you have the added element of being able to change all of those things. So what happens when the car you're following stops being a slow truck and turns into a Ferrari? And what if that Ferrari turns into a garbage truck and tries to crush you?" Interesting questions indeed. Questions Turteltaub and crew were eager to answer.

The chase begins with the Merlinean heroes in Balthazar's fashionable ride of choice, a gleaming,

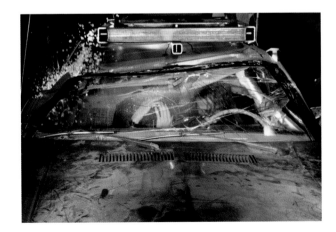

gorgeous 1935 Rolls-Royce Phantom. This magnificent artifact of a truly golden age of motoring turned heads everywhere it filmed in New York. Hundreds of locals and tourists alike posed for photos in front of the vehicle, as if it were one of the stars of the movie.

"We were looking for a great classic car for Balthazar to drive," recalls Jon Turteltaub, "something that had some mystery and magic to it. The Phantom was so perfect. And believe it or not, the engine is actually known as the 'Merlin,' and it also powered the Spitfire airplane, which helped win World War II." Just another one in the "coincidence or magic" category for *The Sorcerer's Apprentice*.

"Most Rolls-Royce cars are special just because they were handmade in limited quantities in England," says Dan Dietrich, who maintained the Phantom throughout production. "But what's special about this one is that it's one of a kind. There are no other vehicles exactly like it. Rolls-Royce made just slightly

TOP LEFT & OPPOSITE: The 1935 Rolls-Royce Phantom in all its gleaming glory. LEFT: A 1976 Pinto is not the place Balthazar and Dave want to be when it's taking a pounding by a garbage truck's lift arm. TOP RIGHT: Balthazar and Dave look happier and safer in a Mercedes McLaren.

more than two thousand Phantoms, and of that, only nineteen were made as coupes, seating only two people. Back then, the cost of an average Rolls-Royce was several times what a house would cost, so to [buy] a coupe, you had to be really wealthy.

"When you purchased a Phantom back in the 1930s," Dietrich goes on to explain, "you basically got an engine and a chassis, and then it was up to you to choose the coach maker to build the body. And what makes this one so special is that the original owner bought the body out of the only Rolls-Royce dealership in Montreal, and picked a body that didn't exist before."

The car chase called for picture car coordinator Mike Antunez to acquire a large number of vehicles, including an exact replica of the priceless Phantom. The replica was utilized as a kind of stunt double for the real car for the chase scene and was created by Cinema Vehicle Services in Los Angeles under the supervision of Ray Claridge. "You can't just go out and buy parts off the shelf for it," he explains. "Pretty much everything has to be hand fabricated. We reshaped fenders, and had to completely rebuild the rear body panel. We also reshaped the doors and lengthened the hood."

The process of assembling the replica, Claridge informs, was rather similar to Dr. Frankenstein creating his Monster, cannibalizing various body parts and then, miraculously, animating them. "The beast is kind of a mixture of a few things. The running gear of the chassis is a 2006 Chevrolet crew cab pickup truck,

and it had to have stunt brakes so they can slide it around corners and bounce off trash cans, that sort of thing. The red and black parts of the body started life as a '32 Rolls-Royce four-door sedan, which we've cut down, twisted, and fitted to make it as close as we could to the hero car. We also fit it with a 5.8 liter Chevy engine and seat-belt harnesses to keep the people operating the vehicle safe. You can straighten out sheet metal, but it's a little harder to straighten out a broken bone!"

"The replica is pretty dang good," compliments Dan Dietrich. "It's pretty incredible that it was built in only six weeks."

In the chase scene, which required three weeks of combined first and second unit filming over long and often rainy nights, Balthazar and Dave's sorcery morphs the Phantom into a sleek, modern Mercedes McLaren, and then incongruously (and mistakenly) into

Part IV

a 1976 Pinto. Horvath, on his end, begins the chase in a Mercedes GL500, which transforms first into a New York yellow taxicab, and then into a speedier Ferrari F30, and, finally, into a weirdly threatening garbage truck.

"This is what I mean when I say that this movie is a heck of a ride," laughs Jay Baruchel. "We have a pretty badass car chase in our movie with the fastest, sexiest cars on earth. I get to ride in a Phantom! In the scene, we literally drive through the heart of Midtown Manhattan and right into a mirror world where everything is backward."

"At one point," explains Jon Turteltaub, "one of the cars is going to crash into a giant piece of mirrored glass that is being put into a building for construction. Well, we've seen cars smash through glass and mirrors before, but we haven't seen them go *into* one and cross over to the other side. In the mirror world they enter into, all the signs are backward, left is right, right is left, and how do you get back to the other side? A car chase is tough enough to figure out when everyone is going in the right direction, but when you're in mirror world, it's really crazy."

That wasn't even the craziest part. Closing down lanes over a stretch of ten blocks on Sixth Avenue in Manhattan and controlling both vehicular and pedestrian traffic was an equally crazy challenge for production. But executive producer Barry Waldman was, as usual, pretty much prepared for anything. "When you sign up for your tenth Bruckheimer movie, you kind of know the drill. You suit up, put your five-point harness on, and strap in for the ride.

"Originally, the chase was just two cars racing down or under the FDR Drive," recalls Waldman, "which was a very easy undertaking, because that section of town is also empty at night. But then the scene evolved into the sorcerer chase. And how do we make it fun and interesting? Well, you do that, of course, by shooting in the most congested areas of the city, like Times Square and Sixth Avenue.

"But we're in the business of making magic," Waldman continues. "It took a long time to convince the city to do that, lots of meetings, lots of dinners, lots of conversations. We took an approach of how to do it in the most efficient way, and how to be good partners with the city. Ironically, on the first night of the shoot, it was raining, and the stunt driver at the wheel of the Ferrari hydroplaned into a restaurant right in the middle of Times Square. Thankfully, no one was seriously injured, and we were able to continue filming for another three weeks to complete what's a pretty spectacular sequence."

And, without doubt, a true piece of car-chasing cinematic magic.

The *Fantasia* Sequence

THE SCENE: Trying to hurry for the date with Becky Barnes which he's waited ten years for, Dave Stutler breaks the first rule of sorcery: "Magic is not to be used for personal gain or shortcuts." In an effort to quickly tidy up the lab, Dave begins to manipulate mops, brooms, buckets, and even sponges to perform his chores for him . . . with disastrous results.

BEHIND THE SCENE: "'The Sorcerer's Apprentice' segment from *Fantasia* is one of the greatest works of Disney animation, so we had to be very careful with how we adapted it," says Jerry Bruckheimer. "We didn't want to ruin the magic, but create new magic as a loving homage to the original."

"Paul Dukas' music was the inspiration for the episode in *Fantasia*," Turteltaub explains, "while the original story from the Goethe poem was the inspiration to the music. Our inspiration is the poem, the music, and the original animated 'Sorcerer's Apprentice.' So with an enormous number of people and resources, we're putting together what we hope is a really entertaining, fun experience that takes the essence of Walt Disney's 'Sorcerer's Apprentice' and gives you our version. The scene should be big,

but not bigger than the movie. It should be fun and playful, but not dominate the entire thing. And most importantly, it has to advance the story. It has to be necessary in the movie, it can't stand alone.

"We had a lot of conversations about not doing it at all, knowing that the original 'Sorcerer's Apprentice' piece in *Fantasia* is a perfect piece of film and such a classic, well-known, iconic piece of film," confesses Turteltaub. "But then Jerry and I agreed that we're not really doing *The Sorcerer's Apprentice* unless we do this scene, because it's the essence of the fable, the Goethe poem, the Dukas music, and the Disney animation. It's about a guy who doesn't quite yet know how to control his magic, and in trying to cut corners, loses control . . . over cleaning products."

Jay Baruchel was challenged and honored by the task at hand, but never intimidated. "It's a huge honor, and a tremendous responsibility, to walk in Mickey Mouse's shoes. Those are pretty big shoes to fill, and I wondered how to do my own thing and make it funny without stepping on and moving away from what made that sequence so iconic in the first place. For me to be in this movie, and be allowed to put my stamp and at the same time dearly pay homage to one of

ABOVE & RIGHT: Animation art and production still of Mickey Mouse as the Sorcerer's Apprentice in *Fantasia*. OPPOSITE: Dave frustratingly tries to stop the mayhem as "green guys" portray the mops and brooms in the live-action element of the *Fantasia* sequence filming.

the most beloved sequences in film history, wasn't lost on me. It was an absolute treat, incredibly fun, and I loved having all those mops and brooms kick my butt. It was just magical."

He laughs before adding, "It was hard not to be a kid in that situation, man. I grew up watching that scene in *Fantasia*, so after getting to do my own version of it, I could retire right now."

Part of what gave Baruchel so much impetus and creativity in his own interpretation of the scene was his thoughtful understanding of the tale's essence. "Adam and Eve couldn't help but eat the apple, right? It's the old 'curiosity killed the cat' thing. Trying to find the quickest, easiest way of getting something done is an ambition that we all share, and we've all had that come back to bite us in the butt cheeks, right? The sequence is about somebody trying to cut out the middleman, and paying a huge price for it."

Although Paul Dukas' timeless music will be freshly adapted by composer Trevor Rabin, who has previously scored a dozen films for Jerry Bruckheimer (including Jon Turteltaub's two *National Treasure* hits, along with *Con Air*, *Armageddon*, and *Enemy of the State*), a traditional version of the piece was played on set during the sequence's filming, not only for atmosphere, but also for specific timing purposes. And although the live-action feature version doesn't slavishly mimic the animated original, there are a few slyly intentional direct references, such as the shadow cast on the lab wall by Dave wearing his hoodie, which looks curiously like the one cast by Mickey Mouse in his peaked sorcerer's hat.

Once again, as Jon Turteltaub indicated, creating what the crew called "the *Fantasia* sequence" required the maximum efforts of every department. In fact, unlike Mickey Mouse in the original animation, or Dave Stutler in the film, *nobody* took shortcuts in conjuring optimum magic from the scene. For production designer Naomi Shohan's massive underground lab set at the Bedford Armory, special-effects foreman Mark Hawker and his crew not only had to install fire rods during construction, but a watertight floor as well for the flooding that occurs in the *Fantasia* sequence. "We had to install an entire system of pumps and drains, because it had to be flooded and then drained very quickly for the turnaround on the takes. We had two six-inch diesel pumps flooding thirty thousand gallons of water in through the underground lab sinks, which then reversed to suck the water out, along with eighteen drains. We could fill a foot of water in the large set in about fifteen minutes, and then drain in about the same amount of time."

Jerry Bruckheimer and Jon Turteltaub are nothing if not experienced at water scenes, considering that the entire climax of *National Treasure: Book of Secrets* saw several sets almost completely immersed in thousands of gallons of water. "In a weird way, the terror

Jon Turteltaub, Jay Baruchel, and the crew work in watery conditions in the flooded underground lab set in the Bedford Armory.

of doing the *Fantasia* sequence went away," says Turteltaub, "because we already had a lot of education in terms of what we had to do and how we had to do it. We have the same physical effects crew on *The Sorcerer's Apprentice* as we did on *NT2*, so I felt safe going in. What I was really excited about was that the scene is about storytelling rather than dialogue, so you tell it with action and images."

The highly spontaneous Turteltaub was, however, occasionally frustrated by the painstaking technicalities of the sequence. "Doing anything with visual effects is a slow and intellectual process, and things have to be done with an exactitude that isn't really what I'm com-

fortable with. It takes probably five times as long to shoot each shot as it does normally, and it pushes you in terms of your responsibility. But it's got to be great. It wouldn't be a Jerry Bruckheimer movie if it weren't great. And we can't just do a cute little montage that is just an homage to the earlier Disney animated 'Sorcerer's Apprentice.'"

As always, the copious number of special effects required for the scene combined the work of both the physical- and visual-effects departments. Senior VFX supervisor John Nelson felt the pressure. "When I was young, I was head usher at a movie theater, and one of the movies we showed for about four or five weeks

104

was *Fantasia*," he recalls. "I must have seen the movie a hundred times. The legacy of being able to work and redo something like that in live action is really quite wonderful. I take it very seriously, because I think what the animators did back in the early 1940s was amazing. We have a lot to live up, and we're trying to make the scene beautiful and fantastic, with a deep sense of fun, which is what the original was.

"There will be a lot of fun in this sequence," Nelson continues. "There will be CG brooms, mops, sponges sliding around like kids in a water park. We're thinking of the action as if the objects begin as well-behaved children in a kindergarten, who then spin off into kids who have just eaten a ton of sugar when the teacher has left the room. It's very difficult to combine CG effects with real water, and we're spending a lot of time with Mark Hawker and his department to establish basic realism. The audience will find it more believable because the CG mop interacts with real water. I have a rule that if I can put in one real shot for every eight to ten visual-effect shots, then it keeps everything honest. The highest compliment that we can get paid in our end of the business is if people say, after seeing the final results, 'Well, what did *you* do? It was all real, right?'"

Among the tricks of the trade employed by Nelson were the so-called "green guys," men and women wearing skintight green suits and holding the props that come to life in the sequence. Explains Nelson, "The green guys are the most effective way to anthropomorphize objects and make them move." Adds Adrian De Wet of Double Negative, the London-based VFX company working on the sequence under Nelson, "They're basically there to hold the mops, brooms, sponges, and other props so that we can have it all in. It's good to have something in there that Jon Turteltaub can direct, and for the actors to respond to. First we shoot with the green guys in the shot, and then we do it again without them, so we have it all covered. The reason they wear green suits is because it makes it easier for the compositors to clean them out digitally."

For the green guys, though, there were little moments of inevitable humiliation. The primary task for Thomas Dupont, one of the top stunt players in the industry, in *The Sorcerer's Apprentice* was doubling Nicolas Cage for action considered just too dangerous for a major movie star. (Dupont has a history with other Jerry Bruckheimer movies, including stints on the *Pirates of the Caribbean* trilogy, as well as portraying Hassad, the whip-blade-wielding Hassansin, in *Prince of Persia: The Sands of Time*.) For the *Fantasia* sequence, however, he found himself wearing the green spandex suit and holding a push broom. "Uh, anytime you forget that you're wearing it," noted Dupont ruefully, "one of the crew members is nice enough to remind you."

Dave clings to one of the Tesla coils during an onslaught of cleaning utensils during the *Fantasia* sequence. A glimpse of the green guys can be seen in the image on the left.

Manifestations

THIS PAGE & OPPOSITE: Visual-effects supervisor John Nelson and London-based Double Negative Visual Effects demonstrate, through this progression of conceptual images, how the *Fantasia* sequence transforms from the green guys moving brooms and mops to a magical cavalcade of objects moving of their own will.

New York City: The *Magic* Is All Around You

"This city is full of magic, if you know where to look," says Balthazar Blake to Dave Stutler, who is approximately a thousand years younger than his ageless mentor and hasn't quite yet learned to open his eyes or his mind to what surrounds him.

There may be no truer words spoken in *The Sorcerer's Apprentice*. For its adoring inhabitants and millions of visitors, New York is truly a city like none other. Its beauty, power, energy, and resilience are monuments to an indomitable spirit that is utterly inclusive, attracting not only the tired, poor, and huddled masses of the Emma Lazarus poem "The New Colossus," which is inscribed on a plaque inside of the Statue of Liberty, but also the rich and the poor, of every race. Now they inhabit—more or less peacefully—the five boroughs that comprise the Eternal City of the New World.

New York has, of course, been the backdrop and location for countless films such as J. Stuart Blackton's *The Thieving Hand* in 1908 and D.W. Griffith's gritty crime drama *The Musketeers of Pig Alley* in 1912. But all too often, other metropolises have been utilized as stand-ins for the real thing, from Toronto to Los Angeles to Sydney. For *The Sorcerer's Apprentice*, however, Jerry Bruckheimer and Jon Turteltaub were determined that the film would shoot nowhere else, and except for a one-day foray across the Hudson River to Jersey City, all eighty-eight days were shot in either Manhattan or Brooklyn. "At one

point," notes executive producer Barry Waldman, "we had thought about shooting all of the exteriors in New York and do interiors in California. I had just finished a movie in New York, so I knew what we could do here. I gave all the pros and cons to Jerry and Jon, and they felt that since

ABOVE: Brooding New York skyline illustration by Tani Kunitake. OPPOSITE: Balthazar emerges from the entrance of a classic Upper West Side apartment building.

New York is really a character in the movie, shooting the entire movie here would make the most sense."

Ironically, but somehow appropriately, most of the stars and key behind-the-camera creative artists on the film were *not* native New Yorkers,

which allowed them to see the city through eyes that were fresh and appreciative.

"New York has everything," says the Detroit-born Jerry Bruckheimer, "wonderful high-rises, a fast pace, the greatest restaurants and clubs in the world, the centers of publishing and finance. And it will never look as magical as it will in *The Sorcerer's Apprentice*."

"The big conceptual idea for the movie," notes Jon Turteltaub, a native of Los Angeles, "is that sorcerers and sorcery are alive and well in the present day, and what more different context than New York City for what we think [of] as an ancient art? It's here, it's present, and one of the things we learned on the *National Treasure* movies is that it's much more entertaining to show audiences the magic in things they recognize than just to create something fake. New York City is an extraordinary place, and New Yorkers are so busy achieving, they often don't actually notice what is here. If you stop and look around, there are amazing things everywhere. If you walk through Manhattan one day, and instead of looking straight ahead, you looked up instead, you will see the most amazing architectural details on those buildings. New York is an entire universe."

But within that universe, Turteltaub also sees two distinct sides. "New York has two kinds of magic," he notes. "One is that you feel like it's a place where anything can be achieved. But there's also a sinister magic to New York. A person is

Filming at the famed art deco statue of Atlas in Rockefeller Center.

Montrealer Jay Baruchel. "In the film, when we're driving along Times Square or Sixth Avenue in the car chase, we're actually doing it. And not only are we shooting in a great city, but Naomi Shohan has created the greatest sets on earth for us. Everybody, including my mother, has been blown away, gobsmacked, and awestruck by the size, grandeur, and detail. People are going to see our movie and get taken away into a New York that they recognize, but [have] never really seen before."

Baruchel also got a kick out of shooting at New York University in Greenwich Village for very particular reasons. "It was amazing for me, because I'd always dreamt of going to NYU Film School and could never float the bill. And there I was getting paid to be there, instead of spending money. Seriously, shooting at NYU was a thrill. So many great movies have come as a result of that institution, and it's so seared into the collective consciousness."

"It's an incredibly photogenic city," notes London-born Alfred Molina, "and has such a dramatic presence and throbbing life. New York becomes another character in The Sorcerer's Apprentice. When the magic happens, it happens in a city that is magical in itself, so there's a double whammy."

"I've never spent much time in New York before," admits Australia-born Teresa Palmer, "but there is a magical energy here that just feels so alive and energetic. It's the sort of city where dreams really do come true, and I think the film definitely lends itself to that." Says Toby Kebbell, "Although New York is so much younger than London, where I live, you can have all these amazing things going on right in front of your face, and you just brush it off because with all of the millions of people milling about, your brain doesn't even register them."

"The goal of this movie," says director of photography Bojan Bazelli, who originally hails from far-off Serbia, "is to create The Sorcerer's Apprentice [version of] New York. We are not trying to particularly change the look of the city, we are embracing it, and then blending it with our own magical vision. The energy between light and dark is in almost every shot, and we used the latest technology and most creative people to give audiences a New York that's fresh, different, and alive with magic."

One sure sign that The Sorcerer's Apprentice was truly a made-in-New York movie was the frequent presence of a gentleman known as "Radioman." The offbeat Radioman, so called because of the large vintage boom box he always wears around his neck, is an icon of the New York movie world, a ubiquitous figure on film sets and other entertainment-related events in the Big Apple. The bearded, somewhat gnarled Radioman knows everyone in the industry, and receives a fair amount of love back in return. And Radioman most certainly got some love from Jon Turteltaub, who, as many other directors have in the past, cast him in a bit part that almost seems to validate the production's presence in the Big Apple. Not to mention quite appropriate, considering that radio was actually invented by Nikola Tesla, a guiding spirit of the entire enterprise.

always a little afraid or cautious in New York. There are so many old buildings, you have to wonder what's gone on in them over the years. There's an underbelly, and so much can be happening out of sight."

"Anyone who's spent any time in New York knows that it is truly the world's capital," states

Of course, shooting in "the city" has its challenges, including horrific vehicular and human traffic, which presented innumerable challenges to first assistant director Geoff Hansen, second AD Pete Thorell, and their hardworking team. But the astounding range of real locations, and the history behind them, took the company's breath away on a consistent basis. In addition to locales discussed elsewhere, such as Bowling Green and the Financial District, Chinatown, the Cathedral of St. John the Divine, Times Square, and Midtown Manhattan, other filming sites included:

- Washington Square Park in Greenwich Village and the exterior of the New York University complex.
- Tribeca, where production designer Naomi Shohan created the exterior of the Arcana Cabana in the 1869 Grosvenor Building on White Street, lined with similar cast-iron buildings from the nineteenth century.
- The Seventh Avenue subway station in

Brooklyn's Park Slope neighborhood, for a scene in which Dave tries to use his new powers of sorcery to overcome an attempting mugging while he's with Becky.
- The Apthorp Apartments on Manhattan's Upper West Side, built in 1903 by William Waldorf Astor, one of the city's richest and most legendary grandees.
- The Bryant Park Hotel on 40th Street, originally the American Standard Building, designed by Raymond M. Hood and J. Andre Fouilhoux and built in 1924 utilizing black brick trimmed with gold-stone ornamentation and Gothic-style pinnacles (some of which was re-created at Bedford Armory as the setting of Drake Stone's penthouse apartment).
- The Williamsburg Bridge, a suspension bridge opened in 1903, which connects Brooklyn with the Lower East Side of Manhattan.
- Battery Park on Manhattan's lowest edge, with the Statue of Liberty looming in the harbor just beyond.
- The actual Chrysler Building (in addition to the set of the sixty-first-story parapet constructed in the Bedford Armory), William Van Alen's Art Deco masterpiece.
- Floyd Bennett Field in the outer reaches of Brooklyn, the first municipal airport in New York City, opened in 1931, which saw the exploits of such great aviators as Amelia Earhart, Wiley Post, Howard Hughes, and Major John Glenn Jr.

ABOVE: Jay Baruchel and Teresa Palmer get soaked to the skin in a special-effects downpour (nothing fake about the wet) at NYU. BELOW LEFT: Jon Turteltaub chats with an uncostumed Alfred Molina in Washington Square Park while, behind, fans look on, eager to get a glimpse of the stars.

- Rockefeller Center, the glorious 1930s complex, with filming adjacent to Lee Lawrie and Rene Paul Chambellan's 1937, fifteen-foot-tall statue, *Atlas*, which is directly across the street from St. Patrick's Cathedral.
- A lecture hall at Brooklyn College, standing in for NYU (which is seen in the film's exterior photography).

For those who work and make their home in New York City, the above are just spots they pass as they go about their days. A commuter from Brooklyn might find it hard to believe the Seventh Avenue subway station in Park Slope, with its dark walls and subterranean feel, could be magical. But in the world of film . . . and sorcery . . . you just never know. And for the cast and crew of *The Sorcerer's Apprentice*, New York City was a humble and exciting leading actor.

Battle at Bowling Green

THE SCENE: For the climax of *The Sorcerer's Apprentice*, all roads led to Bowling Green, the historic park in Lower Manhattan. There, the ultimate high *midnight* showdown occurs between Merlineans Balthazar Blake and Dave Stutler, and Morganian Maxim Horvath. In his evil attempt to destroy Blake once and for all, Horvath conjures up the greatest evil of them all from the Grimhold . . . Morgana herself. Possessing the body of Veronica (Monica Bellucci), the sorceress beloved by both Balthazar and Horvath, Morgana is hell-bent on revenge. What she wants most, after the world, is to inhabit her own body (played in film by actress Alice Krige). The result is the ultimate sorcerer's duel, involving spells, incantations, raging fires, and even the famed *Charging Bull* statue brought to terrifying life by Horvath. The stakes in this battle? Merely the survival of the world itself.

BEHIND THE SCENE: "Once again, a truly iconic New York location was selected for the so-called 'final battle,'" says Jerry Bruckheimer. "Bowling Green was literally the first park ever created in the United States. It's where New Yorkers pulled down the statue of King George during the American Revolution. It's a beautiful circle of greenery in Lower Manhattan surrounded by skyscrapers, and a very dramatic locale for this sorcerer's battle royale."

In fact, Central Park was originally considered as the site for the final battle, but as Bruckheimer points out, "when you're in the middle of Central Park, it could almost be anywhere because it's such a huge expanse of greenery. For our specific purposes, Bowling Green seemed more dramatic because it's a relatively confined green space surrounded by impressive old New York skyscrapers. It's almost like an arena in which the action could be played out."

ABOVE: Costume designer Michael Kaplan's concept for Morgana, illustrated by Brian Valenzuela. OPPOSITE: Early illustration of the Morgana separation by Craig Mullins.

"Morgana, the greatest and most powerful sorceress, was thrust into the Grimhold and imprisoned," explains Jon Turteltaub. "But in order to get her in there, a Merlinean sorceress named Veronica gave up her own soul, so both Morgana and Veronica are stuck together in this Grimhold. Balthazar Blake has been madly in love with Veronica for more than a thousand years. But to let her out he has to let Morgana out as well, and that's part of the sacrifice of being a Merlinean. If Morgana is set free, he will get his love back, but the world may be destroyed. So the question facing Balthazar is how can he destroy Morgana and not destroy Veronica?" It is this complex question, or compulsion, that leads to the final battle.

The challenges facing Bruckheimer, Turteltaub, and company in the filming of the final battle were legion, beginning with something utterly beyond their control: Mother Nature. The second-wettest June in the history of New York City was the June of 2009, with 10.06 inches of rain nearly matching the 10.27-inch record.

So when did the final battle begin filming? Conveniently, it began Friday, June 5, and completed on Thursday, June 25. Each shooting day was a tough slog of an all-nighter, with cast and crew dodging downpours and drizzle. "It seemed to never stop raining," recalls executive producer Barry Waldman. "But the city helped us organize a plan in order to be in Bowling Green for what was originally scheduled as a ten-day sequence for first unit, followed by second unit work. The biggest decision that we made was to switch the workweek from Wednesday through Sunday, because down here in the Financial District, most businesses are closed on the weekend. That enabled us to take over Bowling Green for Friday, Saturday, and Sunday nights without disrupting business."

For the company, it was clearly an honor to be permitted to film inside America's first public park, so declared in 1733 by the Common Council, primarily for the popular sport of lawn bowling (hence its name). On July 9, 1776, after a copy of the Declaration of Independence arrived from Philadelphia and was read on Broadway, colonists toppled the four-thousand-pound equestrian statue of King George III found in the park, chopped it to bits, and melted it

down for ammunition with which to fight the British. The elegant town houses that once surrounded the park were replaced in the early twentieth century by impressive edifices that housed the offices of some of the world's greatest shipping lines, including the United States Lines-Panama Pacific Lines at One Broadway, the White Star Line (parent company of the *Titanic*) at 11 Broadway, and the Cunard Building at 25 Broadway (to be used by *The Sorcerer's Apprentice* for remarkable purposes described in the next section of the book).

The city also allowed production designer Naomi Shohan and her art department team to temporarily convert a fountain in the middle of Bowling Green into a larger structure, which included, once again, the installation of flame bars to create a ring of fire. "We laid down the pipes for the fire in the fountain,"

notes special-effects foreman Mark Hawker, "so that we could fully encircle Morgana in the flames. John Nelson and his VFX department then take the flames that we create and do runners that go up the buildings to create [a] giant Merlin Circle. In the fountain, we also have bubblers and steam, and had to rig Primacord for explosions."

For the ring of fire, Hawker and his team used sixteen short flame bars, with fourteen forty-three-pound propane tanks to feed them. "It's all set up so that you light the first one, and then there are basically wall switches, each one controlling another twelve inches of fire. We can go either clockwise, counterclockwise, do all sorts of patterns." It was important, though, that the special-effects team not incinerate international star Monica Bellucci, who needed to be right in the middle of that ring of fire. "A two-foot

flame by itself isn't bad," notes Hawker, "but when you have an entire ring of them, it's sucking in toward the center and it gets very, very hot in there."

Monica Bellucci, however, was focused on other matters. "When I'm in front of the camera, I'm just thinking about acting. I don't think very much about the special effects. I know that when I see the movie it's going to be a big surprise for me. During the final battle I had so much fun imagining that I had fire coming out from my hands. And I was confident about this beautiful team that had been working on the movie for so long before I arrived. I felt very secure and protected."

The sequence certainly gave the usually unflappable stunt coordinator George Marshall Ruge some unwanted stress both before and during its filming. "The final battle kept getting pushed on the schedule as it underwent a substantial metamorphosis through evolving script pages," explains Ruge. "Obviously, it was a very important sequence that had to serve as the climax to the story, along with the resolution to numerous character relationships. There was so much to accomplish in a single sequence, along with the physical action that had to be unique, while melding into the fabric of the story.

"We received final script changes literally *days* before the sequence was to shoot," continues Ruge. "Most departments were scrambling to react to last-minute details and changes, and there was significant anxiety. The location of Bowling Green contributed to the problems we had to overcome. The physical action required some wirework and ratchets, but we were limited in what we could do. We could not use cranes because of location restrictions, and the shooting grid was surrounded by trees, which made pick points and wire placement difficult. And since the sequence was shot at night over a number of days, this dictated that any testings and rehearsals had to be accomplished during daylight and very public hours.

"The biggest test," Ruge goes on, "became the moment in which Balthazar is propelled out of the Bowling Green and into the plaza outside of the [park] gates by Horvath. We had to test this with sandbags,

followed by a physical rehearsal with a stunt double. Because we couldn't use a full-size crane, we had to use a small crane arm, which would fit onto the plaza. This dictated a lower pick point for the wires that were used to 'fly' the double, which in turn dictated a low flight between a row of park benches and up to, but not impacting, an iron fence and gate. This was a very difficult piece of action to pull off. We had one six-hour daylight pre-call to dial this in, and had to work around the throng of people who frequent Bowling Green on any given day. As the night and shooting crew call approached, we had some very anxious moments with failed attempts before it finally came together minutes before we had to shut things down. I ended up shooting this particular action on second unit with multiple cameras, and it went perfectly on each of two takes."

The stunt department wasn't the only one taxed

by the demands of the final battle. "This is the most challenging sequence in the movie for our visual-effects department," said a rather exhausted John Nelson as the sequence neared the end of its filming, "because it incorporates the stars, stunt players, lots of visual effects, character animation, and bringing a famous statue of a bull to life, flipping cars and chasing Balthazar Blake all over Bowling Green. It's also where we had to create the final Merlin Circle over the entire top level of the tip of Manhattan. This is where there's a huge sorcerer fight, with lots of plasma bolts being fired in all directions."

The bull of which Nelson speaks is the famed *Charging Bull*, the seven-thousand-pound bronze sculpture by Sicilian-born New Yorker Arturo Di Modica which proudly stands at the tip of Bowling Green. It is, without doubt, one of Manhattan's most beloved and photographed attractions. The very emblem of aggressive Wall Street optimism, the magnificent sculpture already looks as if it's in movement, with its flared nostrils, rippling muscles, and coiled tail. Thousands of tourists a day visit *Charging Bull*, taking photos and treating it as interactive public art, with adults and children alike climbing atop like rodeo riders.

Charging Bull has a history that, though not as lengthy as that of the historic park in which it's positioned, is fascinating in its own right. Arturo Di Modica created the sculpture entirely on his own accord, without a commission, two years after the 1987 stock market crash as a symbol of the enduring spirit of the American people. He installed it on December 15, 1989, in front of the New York Stock Exchange as a gift to the people of the city, only to have the police seize and impound the sculpture. But the public responded with howls of support for Di Modica and his truly public artwork, and community

Illustration by Tani Kunitake of Arturo Di Modica's *Charging Bull* sculpture, activated into terrifying life.

118

The infamous "car flipper," operated by Mark Hawker and his team, brings to life the scene in which Balthazar must outrun the angry bull (which will be added later by visual-effects supervisor John Nelson and Double Negative Visual Effects).

leader Arthur Piccolo stepped in, arranging with the sculptor and New York City Department of Parks and Recreation Commissioner Henry J. Stern to move *Charging Bull* two blocks south to the plaza in front of Bowling Green. *Charging Bull* was welcomed to its new home in Bowling Green on December 20, 1989, which was quite a Christmas present to the city, its citizens, and visitors from around the world. And just as the Chrysler eagle was magically brought to life by the filmmakers, *Charging Bull* was about to receive similar transformational treatment.

"On second unit," says George Marshall Ruge, "we covered Balthazar's action with the bull, chasing him from the plaza and out into the street, where [the animal] flips two cars high in the air as it tries to get to its 'prey.' We had Nic, but we did not have what would become the CG bull in postproduction. Nic was absolutely fantastic in pulling this off and acting with his unseen nemesis. Without his great performance, it would have been impossible to pull this off with any credibility. The flipping of the cars was extremely time-consuming in terms of setting the mechanics of

doing this with practical special effects, and the multiple cameras for each setup. The night became long, we were fighting the fast-approaching dawn, and shot right up to and a bit beyond sunrise. We made our day, but I don't think many on the crew were able to go home and right to sleep after sprinting all night to get this done."

"Working with John Nelson," says Mark Hawker, "we tried to do as much physical effects as possible. Obviously, the bull isn't actually going to actually come alive and run down the street—that's John's territory—but we're responsible for objects that are being moved by the digitalized bull. There's a moment when the bull flips some cars, so we have the famous car flippers for that. We do the implosion and the flip at the same time, which will give the effect of the bull sticking its head inside the car, crushing it, and then flinging it off his horns."

A car *what*???

"A car flipper," explains Hawker, "is a ten-inch pneumatic cylinder that operates on very high pressure. It's almost like putting a deck of cards on top of a mousetrap. If you trip it, the cards are going to flip up in the air. It's kind of the same principal, on a much larger scale. We also flew some metal newspaper dispenser boxes, which also get knocked around by

the bull, using pneumatic cylinders and guide cables. It looks out of control when the boxes are flying toward Balthazar, but it was really very carefully guided."

For his part, John Nelson wanted to make certain that his digitalized charging bull hewed as closely as possible to the original sculpture. "The first thing I did was walk up to the statue in the middle of the night when no one else was there, and started taking photo details of angles that I liked: over the horns, under the feet, wide sides to show how big it is. Then I went back and showed those to Jon Turteltaub and Bojan Bazelli, our director of photography. We then built a surrogate of the bull, which we attached to c-stands—metal stands used by grips to hold lights and flags—so that Jon and Bojan could see where the digital bull is going to be in the shot.

Nelson continues, "We also cast a one-eighth-scale bull front that one of our crew could wear, and go through the motions that the digital bull will be doing, so that we can see the action, and also detect how the light plays off the scale model bull."

Admittedly, this was a fairly comical sight for the hordes of spectators that gathered for their evening's entertainment by watching the movie goings-on both inside of and, occasionally, outside of the Bowling Green fence. Bojan Bazelli had his gaffers, Tony "Nako" Nakonechnyj and Michael Gallart, float two massive lighting balloons above the park that made it look from a few blocks away like UFOs were invading Manhattan. Residents and tourists exiting the nearby ferries to Staten Island or the Statue of Liberty and Ellis Island were astonished to find themselves on the set of a major Hollywood movie, particularly when Nicolas Cage would suddenly wade into their midst to sign autographs and exhaustively pose for photos.

But more than once, the poor production assistant wearing the scaled-down bull front would audibly pick up a humiliating "Olé!" from the crowd. Well, that's the glamour of show business.

119

THIS PAGE & OPPOSITE: Together at last, Balthazar and his love, Veronica, have only a brief reunion before they must face off against Morgana (Alice Krige) and Horvath.

ALCHEMY

Walking *Between* Worlds

LEFT: Panoramic illustration by Dean Tschetter of the Chrysler Building parapet. CENTER: Jon Turteltaub works on set with production designer Naomi Shohan (center) and script supervisor Julie Pitkanen (left). RIGHT: Tani Kunitake's early conceptual illustration of the Dark Ages for a flashback sequence.

PRODUCTION DESIGN

"Naomi Shohan is amazing," says Jerry Bruckheimer of the woman who was given the weighty task of designing *The Sorcerer's Apprentice*. "Her work in *I Am Legend* was fantastic, and she has even more leeway in this film because we're in a magical world."

Shohan's body of work reveals both great range and enormous imagination. Her other films have trafficked from gritty realism (*Feeling Minnesota*, *Tears of the Sun*, *Training Day*), to flights of imagination (*Constantine*, *I Am Legend*), to a combination of both (*American Beauty*, *The Lovely Bones*).

For *I Am Legend*, Shohan converted New York City into a deserted, postapocalyptic landscape in which huge tracts of the city have returned to the natural growth of the forests and dales from whence it came.

For *The Sorcerer's Apprentice*, she not only highlights the already iconic magnificence of the city, but goes deeper and finds the hidden magic as well. "In the early stages, we talked about insinuating that there has always been a presence of sorcery in Manhattan," says Shohan, "and we talked about where we might find that. In Manhattan, you walk around and come upon these miraculous buildings everywhere you look, just out of nowhere. Or miraculous interiors as you go about your sort of mundane business. So, I was hoping to establish a kind of undercurrent of possibility.

"The Victorian buildings from the turn of the twentieth century were particularly beautiful, and they have a poetry about them that lends itself beautifully to sorcery," Shohan continues. "Other sets have to do with the infrastructure *under* Manhattan, which was being built in the late 1800s and into the early 1900s, which we incorporate in the underground training lab set. I tried to create atmosphere that's at once realistic and has to do with a kind of grubby, visceral feeling of New York City, the shoulder-rubbing, intense density of it all. In New York you can walk down the street, open a door, and find yourself in a new world . . . so I liked the idea that you walk between worlds."

In addition to choosing the "practical" locations with the filmmakers, Shohan also designed sets of extraordinary detail that were constructed either inside of soundstages at Steiner Studios (site of the former Brooklyn Navy Yard) or within the gargantuan and suitably spooky confines of the 1907 Bedford Armory, also in Brooklyn.

Underground Lab/
Sorcerer Training Room

The massive, meticulously detailed underground lab/sorcerer training room set is the site of some of the film's most important sequences, including the *Fantasia* sequence, and was unquestionably Shohan's most ambitious structure created for the film.

"In the script, the lab where Dave Stutler conducts his experiments was described as a basement room somewhere," explains Naomi Shohan. "From that, I extrapolated that it could be really deep underground, because he's working with incredible high-voltage equipment, which needs a protective space. Earth is the best insulator, and New York really does have some amazing subterranean spaces that are usually off-limits. For example, about one hundred fifty feet beneath Grand Central Station there's a switching station which dates from the World War Two era. Under City Hall there's an incredibly beautiful subway station that's out of use, arched, and very elegant. And

beneath Brooklyn there are old railway tracks from the 1800s, which were used to bring goods to the center of Brooklyn for distribution after picking them up at the docks. So for the underground lab set, we used the idea of subterranean New York in the old days, when there was service between port and commercial centers. And the set needed to be interesting enough to sustain many scenes that were required to be shot inside of it."

What Naomi Shohan created was an old subway turnaround, beautifully redolent of ghostly old New York, converted into a makeshift laboratory. Its interior is graced with an arched and tiled-dome ceiling, cast-iron walkways and staircases, and rusted old elevators. As it is Dave's lab, the interior is tricked out with scientific paraphernalia that resembles something dragged out of the old *Bride of Frankenstein* lab: Tesla coils, a plasma generator, cages filled with obsolete scientific materials, two huge, rusted generators, Jurassic-age computers with reel-to-reel

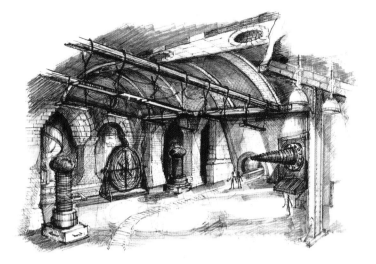

disks, and other detritus of the generations.

So authentic was the carefully aged and weathered environment that many visitors to the set actually thought that it was carved right out of the armory walls. A construction crew under coordinator Ronald Petagna built the set in fourteen weeks, a remarkable feat considering its size and incredible detail. Shohan very deliberately wanted the lab to subtly echo the castle-like setting of Walt Disney's *Fantasia*. "The shape of the set is reminiscent of a castle keep, with very large stones at the bottom of the arches. The iron staircase we built takes the place of the stone staircase in the Mickey Mouse version. When the water engulfs the set in the *Fantasia* sequence, Balthazar enters from the top of the stairs and puts an end to the chaos, just as the old sorcerer did in 'The Sorcerer's Apprentice' segment in *Fantasia*."

Another crucial piece of Shohan's design for the underground lab was the Merlin Circle with its seven domains—Space-Time, Motion, Matter, Elements, Transformation, Mind, and, most importantly, in the center, the Forbidden Domain/Love—which Balthazar conjures up from the cobblestoned floor of the lab. Shohan and her team did considerable research, even consulting a genuine Wiccan to figure out the symbols.

Two illustrations of Naomi Shohan's wondrous underground training room, by Barbara Matis (above) and Dean Tschetter (left).

The Arcana Cabana

The Arcana Cabana

"One of the coolest sets in the movie is the Arcana Cabana," affirms Jon Turteltaub, "which is a store of antiquities, obscurities, oddities, and all the things that Balthazar's collected over his millennia of existence. In our head, it was sort of like the Staples of sorcery, so that when a guy says, 'Oh, I need a special ring, some special dust, and the eye of a newt,' he went to the Arcana Cabana."

"The iron architecture of late nineteenth and early twentieth centuries is, I think, some of the most beautiful in New York," notes Naomi Shohan. "I thought that it was the kind of space you would want for the Arcana Cabana. There were a lot of greenhouses built that way in England, and the thought was that Balthazar had moved from Britain to the United States perhaps one or two hundred years before, and perhaps the interior of the Arcana Cabana would reflect some of his former home."

While housed in the Steiner Studios, the glorious interior of the Arcana Cabana features the kind of late nineteenth century New York design that makes architecture buffs salivate: staunch cast-iron beams, an old elevator, a skylight faded with the patina of age, and—thanks to set decorator George DeTitta, Jr.— spilling over with no fewer than half a million assorted objects of escalating weirdness, including old books, tribal masks, lamps, a prosthetic leg, disembodied dolls' heads, shrunken heads, musical instruments, hat and shoe boxes, medicine bottles, skeletons, a unicorn skull, musical instruments, statues, old magician posters, paintings, clocks, framed photos from days of yore, and, oh yes, a sorcerer's hat that looks just like something once worn by a certain famous mouse. A Merlin Circle greets customers of the Arcana Cabana on the floor just before the main entrance, a certain sign that more mysteries lie within if they're wise enough to understand the magical implications.

TOP: A Gregory Hill illustration of Naomi Shohan's Arcana Cabana interior. ABOVE: Examples of George DeTitta, Jr.'s inventive set decoration.

ABOVE & BELOW: Dean Tschetter's illustrations of Naomi Shohan's delightfully over-the-top designs for Drake Stone's penthouse. RIGHT: In a hilarious twist on a painting by Ingres, Gregory Hill presents Drake Stone as he undoubtedly pictures himself.

Drake Stone's Penthouse

Actor Toby Kebbell may be honored by the knowledge that Naomi Shohan actually designed the penthouse lair of his character, illusionist/Morganian/egoist Drake Stone, after first seeing him perform in the role. "I was in Chinatown shooting one night in the freezing cold next to boxes of smelly fish," she recalls, "when in walked Toby in costume, hair, and makeup as Drake Stone for Jerry Bruckheimer and Jon Turteltaub's approval. It was just the most delightful vision. Toby is very good-natured, and plays a wonderful buffoon, taking his narcissism to the extreme. His character inspired me to think of what kind of environment such a man would live in, so we came up with an over-the-top expression of glorious male pomposity."

Drake Stone's domicile looks like a demented Vegas high roller's fantasy of the perfect penthouse, with its creamy walls and overly lavish furniture, insanely huge fireplace with a bust of Drake Stone himself looming just above the mantel, mounted samurai armor, grandiose paintings (with Drake Stone as the worshipful centerpiece), posters of past shows starring the illusionist, and "chandeliers that probably

cost more than any of us make in ten years," as Shohan laughingly describes them. In Stone's study, there are artifacts of illusionists past, including Harry Houdini's famous water chamber, as well as a full-size guillotine and iron maiden, dummy heads, and, for the kiddies, various Drake Stone consumer products (i.e., activity books, breakfast cereal, skateboards, a video game, and children's costumes).

"Originally, we tried to find a real environment for Drake's penthouse," notes supervising art director David Lazan, "but there was nothing that quite worked in terms of scale and scope. And for the action sequence that takes place within the space, to try and make that work in a practical environment didn't seem feasible. Finally, the producers signed off on building a set at the Bedford Armory, which solved all of the problems." If only everything were that easy.

127

Alchemy

Dave Stutler's Apartment

"It seemed like Dave should live in squalor," says Naomi Shohan, "but in a place where he could see the glittering skyline of Manhattan. So I took the subway into Brooklyn, to Williamsburg, and when you get off at the first stop—Marcy Avenue—there are apartment buildings that are practically on top of the tracks. And as I walked down the steps from the train station onto the street, I sort of glanced over and there was a guy sitting in his window at eye level to me, typing away on his laptop. He glanced at me, and I thought, 'Oh my God, that's Dave.'

"It just seemed such a strong choice to have him where trains go by every five minutes," Shohan continues, "because there's something very challenging about living like that. It gave him a very off-the-grid kind of character. But from the vantage of his apartment, Dave could see the city and where his life is going to transform."

Dave's diminutive apartment, with an adjacent hallway and stairs, was built in the same soundstage at Steiner Studios, which housed the Arcana Cabana interior and was realistic enough so that the cast and crew had to wedge themselves and their equipment into the tight spaces. Just outside the windows was an exact replica of the stairs leading up to the Marcy Avenue subway station in Williamsburg. All that was missing was the actual rumble of the trains careening down the tracks.

Production designer Naomi Shohan's and set decorator George DeTitta, Jr.'s extremely proletarian interior for Dave Stutler's apartment and the tenement building that contains it.

ABOVE: Calcutta, circa 1847, as illustrated by Tani Kunitake. This would later come to life under Naomi Shohan's supervision in the 1919 Cunard Building in lower Manhattan.
OVERLEAF: Dean Tschetter's illustration of the Chinese herbalist shop, which was wonderfully brought to life on a set at the Bedford Armory.

Travel to Other Lands and Other Times

Naomi Shohan, supervising art director David Lazan, and their art department colleagues also designed numerous other environments constructed in the cavernous Bedford Armory, including a Chinatown acupuncturist shop—the site of an action-packed sorcerer's encounter between Balthazar and Horvath—so atmospheric and detailed you could literally smell the herbs and traditional medicines; and an incredibly realistic replica of the sixty-first-floor parapet of the Chrysler Building, as well as the NYU men's room, the site of yet another sorcerer's battle, built at Steiner Studios.

But Shohan also utilized some nonstudio structures in New York for her brilliant sets. Remarkably, looking at the massive Great Hall of the 1919 Cunard Building at 25 Broadway, almost directly across the street from Bowling Green in Lower Manhattan, she saw Calcutta, circa 1847.

At one time the ticket office for the classic steamship company, the space has changed from when architect Benjamin Wistar Morris and muralist Ezra Winter produced a decorative program focused on shipping themes and set it within a huge vaulted space that recalls ancient Roman bathhouses. For the prologue of *The Sorcerer's Apprentice*, in which Balthazar Blake combs the world through the ages in search of his apprentice, Shohan transformed the Great Hall into a nineteenth-century Indian marketplace, covered with dirt and dust, replete with trees and other greenery, thatched or canvas-covered market stalls selling baskets, spices, fabrics, fruit, and birds, with bamboo scaffolding and colorful saris drying on clotheslines.

Animals brought into the hall included a monkey, goats, and a magnificent, purebred seventeen-year-old Brahma bull named Bandit. Nearly two hundred extras, most of them recruited from New York City's huge Indian or Indian-American (or Pakistani) community, were outfitted by costume designer Michael Kaplan in an appropriately fantastic array of saris, dhotis, and turbans, with some background players of European extraction portraying red-coated British soldiers and other assorted colonialists. Passersby just outside the doors of 25 Broadway looked on in wonderment as the exotically arrayed background players filed in and out of the building, or took a break on the front steps in between takes.

Outside, New York City, with its hustle, bustle, traffic, and glorious noise. Inside, the smells of spices, animals, and plants, and the sound of Hindu chanting. It was, as Shohan described, walking between worlds, a surrealistic step over a threshold that instantly time-tripped cast, crew, and background alike.

The very next night, another leap in time and culture, from old India to even older England, as a burnt-out section of the giant Church of St. John the Divine on 110th Street on the Upper West Side was magically converted by Shohan and company into a medieval British marketplace, as well as Veronica's sorcerer laboratory. Dozens of extras in period clothing, including jewelry makers, peddlers, musicians, and their customers, mingled with horses, pigs, goats, dogs, and chickens. Once again, there was the distinct feeling . . . magic was at work.

What the *Best* Sorcerers Wear

LEFT: Tani Kunitake early concept illustration of Morgana. CENTER: Costume designer Michael Kaplan (left) consults with Jon Turteltaub at the Eldridge Street location in Chinatown.
RIGHT: Early concept illustration by Daniel Dos Santos of Balthazar's costume, which was considerably changed by the time the film went into production.

COSTUME DESIGN

"Michael Kaplan is somebody I've worked with for many years, and he has the best taste of anyone in Hollywood," says Jerry Bruckheimer of the costume designer. Kaplan designed the costumes for several of the producer's previous productions, including *Armageddon*, *Pearl Harbor*, and *Flashdance*, the latter profoundly influencing pop fashions of the early 1980s. Kaplan's first feature credit was Ridley Scott's *Blade Runner*, and thereafter he devoted his artistry to such films as David Fincher's *Se7en*, *Fight Club*, and *Panic Room*, Scott's *Matchstick Men* (which

starred Nicolas Cage), *Mr. and Mrs. Smith*, *Miami Vice*, *I Am Legend* (in which Kaplan first collaborated with production designer Naomi Shohan), and just before he began work on *The Sorcerer's Apprentice*, reinventing the iconic costumes of the crew of the U.S.S. *Enterprise* for J.J. Abrams's *Star Trek*.

"The characters in *The Sorcerer's Apprentice* were so much fun," says Kaplan, "and I knew they'd be incredible to dress, and so diversified. There would be contemporary clothes, medieval, Chinese armor, it sounded like I would be doing five different movies. And the appeal of working with Jerry again, and Jon Turteltaub, really piqued my interest. The film has a

heightened level of reality, and I think a lot of kids are going to see the movie, so I wanted each character to have their own color palette and for each one to be recognized immediately not only from their faces, but from what they're wearing."

Naomi Shohan, Michael Kaplan, and their teams all know that no matter how much blood, sweat, and tears may be shed in the course of production—and all three are inevitable by-products of filmmaking—it's all for a common cause. "When you have the best of the best on the job," says Jerry Bruckheimer, "all of their hard work can be seen where it belongs, up on the screen."

Balthazar Blake

"I wanted Balthazar Blake to be mysterious and timeless," explains Kaplan, "kind of a dark figure, even though he's a good guy. I saw him as a shadowy figure, always in the same clothes throughout the movie, kind of like his uniform. I thought about sorcerers and their long robes, and imagined that he should have a long leather coat instead, with a leather vest beneath. I wanted it to have a period feeling but not necessarily any specific period, with elements that he had picked up along the way through the ages, some of them never really seen: a necklace he wears with a lot of amulets from different time periods, keys he could have used in the last century, small lockets with old hand-painted pictures of loved ones he might have left behind, certain stones that bring luck or protection, a shark's tooth in a little pouch and a sun pin he wears on his shoulder, a bracelet with cobalt stones.

"Nicolas Cage was very specific about some of the things he wanted as part of that costume," Kaplan continues. "Balthazar's sorcerer ring, which might date back to the time of Merlin, is a green diamond, the rarest of all diamonds, which Nic feels is empowering. Balthazar wears rings on every finger, and each one was made for Nic, because we needed so many multiples it's not like you can just go out and buy a ring and say, 'I'll have ten of these.' Most of them look ancient, and as if they're from different parts of the world.

"But I didn't want Balthazar to be a character who, when he walks down the street in New York, gets stared at like he was from another planet," Kaplan adds. "He does look a bit eccentric, but by New York standards, it's within the realm of acceptability."

Everyone on set knew when Nicolas Cage—or at least his long coat—was approaching, from the incredibly earthy smell of the leather. Ten exact copies of the coat were handcrafted by artisans in Michael Kaplan's costume workshop (housed in an

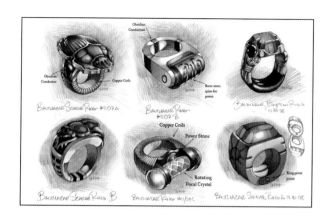

ABOVE: Gregory Hill's illustration of Balthazar's dazzling array of sorcerer rings. BELOW: Property master Jimmy Mazzola models the dragon ring in its sedentary, non-moving incarnation. LEFT TOP: Illustration by Gregory Hill of Michael Kaplan's costume concept for Balthazar Blake. LEFT BOTTOM: Michael Kaplan's costume workshop at Steiner Studios in Brooklyn.

old Quonset hut at Steiner Studios, where Kaplan and his large department of talented cutter-fitters, sewers, milliners, agers/dyers, costumers, and assistants were based), as were myriad other items of clothing, most of which were *not* the kind you buy off the rack!

"Most of the costumes are custom made," says Kaplan, "including the hats. Balthazar's hat was based on a fedora, but we adjusted the height to make it into a quasipeaked sorcerer's hat." It should also be noted that Balthazar's hat is emblazoned with crescent moon and star pins, an obvious tip of the brim to the headwear "Sorcerer Mickey" made famous.

133

134

ABOVE: Michael Kaplan's designs for Dave Stutler's very typical college-age wear, as illustrated by Brian Valenzuela

Dave Stutler & Becky Barnes

"I wanted Dave to seem a little bit of a brilliant but scatterbrained NYU student who was somebody more interested in being a scientist than in clothes," asserts Kaplan. "So his clothes don't necessary always match. Dave has his little uniform of his hoodie, plaid shirt, blue jeans, and sneakers, just stuff that he throws on every day. I wanted it to be cinematic, but not to look like he'd put a lot of time or care into it. We ended up having to make most of Jay Baruchel's clothes, because we needed so many multiples for him, and it's actually more difficult to make clothes like that than if you bought them in an expensive store.

"And Teresa Palmer, who plays Becky, is just so adorable that I just wanted to give her clothes that would enhance what was already there." Becky dresses naturally but with effortless elegance in a not atypical student combination of sweaters, parkas, pants, scarves, blouses, skirts, and boots, all of which looked outrageously attractive on Teresa Palmer.

Maxim Horvath

"One of the things that's great about Maxim Horvath," notes executive producer Mike Stenson, "is that he was imprisoned in the Grimhold during the Roaring Twenties, so when he's released, he's still wearing the bowler hat and spats, looking like he's from a very different era."

"As played by Alfred Molina, Horvath is very dapper, very well dressed, always in beautiful suits and coats," says Michael Kaplan. "I tried to find fabrics that had metallic threads in them. It just added a level of mystique and I thought, perhaps, that his alchemy would work better if there was a fabric that was a conductor of electricity. He has an amazing fur-fringed coat with this material. Men don't wear hats anymore, but when they did, a homburg was always one step below a top hat in terms of dressiness, so Horvath wears a different homburg in each one of his scenes.

ABOVE, LEFT TO RIGHT: Michael Kaplan gave Horvath a debonair look—from his various hats to the elegant cane he wields with great power. Illustration by Gregory Hill.

We have a wonderful milliner named Scott Kopic creating all of the hats by hand. Horvath also has beautiful gloves, cuff links, and, in one scene, spats.

"For Horvath's sorcerer cane, I worked with Jimmy Mazzola, our propmaster. We went through a lot of research looking at period canes, and we chose a few designs that Jimmy then fabricated. We chose the color of the gemstones and metals, and Jimmy did a beautiful job with that."

It seems, for Horvath, the clothes truly made the sorcerer.

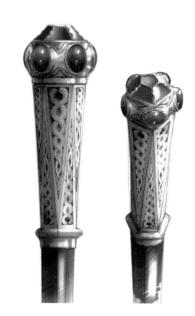

ABOVE: Illustration by Gregory Hill of Horvath's jewel-tipped cane. BELOW: Property master Jimmy Mazzola, on set with the illuminated "hero" version of the cane.

TOP, LEFT TO RIGHT: A few of Drake Stone's outrageous looks (including an illustration by Gregory Hill). ABOVE: Stone's tattoos being applied.

Drake Stone

The same can be said about Toby Kebbell's character. "Drake Stone was so much fun to do," enthuses Kaplan, "and collaborating with Toby Kebbell was wonderful. He was game for pretty much anything. I fashioned him after a few different Las Vegas illusionists, no one in particular, but Drake is more over the top than any of them. He's almost like a rock star of the magician set. He wears beautiful snakeskin pants in one scene, he has tattoos [inside note: one of them is a Hidden Mickey], and also rings on every finger. Everything is emblazoned with his initials, like a bandanna that has a rhinestone 'DS' on it. He also wears this kind of rock-band jacket that looks like something out of *Yellow Submarine*.

"I also thought that another way to make Drake outrageous was to start with his walk," Kaplan goes on. "So I found these shoes made by a friend of mine in Paris named Rick Owens, which are men's boots but with three-inch heels. I thought that Toby was going to say no, but he was game for everything.

"I talked to hair department head Alan D'Angerio before Toby was even cast," Kaplan remembers, "and I thought it would be really great if we could do a spiky blond wig, but to do it so that it looked like his own hair, which Alan achieved by putting black roots on the wig. It kind of added the punk quality to the look, because Drake really doesn't care about his roots showing, and who would ever think that a wig would have black roots?"

Veronica/Morgana

"We see Monica Bellucci as Veronica in three or four different changes," notes Kaplan. "First, there's a contemporary costume when Balthazar thinks he sees her on a New York street, which is a trick that Horvath is playing on him. Then she has two medieval costumes, when she's in the marketplace with Balthazar in happier times, and then the scene in which she is first [released from the Grimhold and shares her body with Morgana]. The lilac medieval dress was actually designed before Monica was cast, but I think sometimes it's better to create a costume for the character and not for the actress. Monica,

however, looks beautiful in it.

"Morgana's costume is probably my favorite in the movie," Kaplan continues. "It's a kind of quilted, shiny black fabric that I found, encrusted with black pearls. We also made these beautiful earrings for her, and she wears these very, very tall shoes under the long, long skirt, which makes her look even taller, and very formidable.

"I wanted to find a way to separate Veronica from Morgana when they weren't separate entities," explains Kaplan, "so I came up with this idea to do mirrored contact lenses for Monica Bellucci which she wears when Veronica is possessed by Morgana."

TOP: Gregory Hill's illustration of Morgana. LEFT: Veronica goes from a Gregory Hill drawing to the real thing in an outfit designed by Michael Kaplan and inspired by the fashion of medieval England. ABOVE: Monica Bellucci's astonishing mirrored eyes.

137

Alchemy

138

Sun Lok

"I really loved doing the Sun Lok character," Kaplan confesses. "I kept asking Jon Turteltaub if he was going to cast somebody young and fit, because I felt that we had seen lots of ancient Chinese sorcerers in other movies, and I didn't want to do a costume that was a cliché. We thought it would be great if Sun Lok was young, vital, and more of a warrior. Even though Sun Lok's metal armored skirt was pretty accurate— we did lots of research—the rest of the costume was

LEFT: Illustration by Brian Valenzuela of Michael Kaplan's fantastical costume for Sun Lok. ABOVE & RIGHT: Gregory Woo, as Sun Lok, shows off Kaplan's creation. Note the red CGI markings on the metal breastplate, which will be replaced by a dragon ornament that springs to life in the film.

a little bit of a departure from reality. I just had a lot of fun, and Gregory Woo, who was cast as Sun Lok, was so excited about playing the character that he was willing to go along with what we did in tandem with Bernadette Mazur's makeup and Alan D'Angerio's hair departments. He had very long hair, and we shaved his head except in the center, so that he had kind of a horse's tail growing from the top of his head. He also wore contact lenses that were almost entirely white with just a little black dot in the center.

"We first see Sun Lok as a butterfly morphs into a beautiful Chinese robe that he's wearing. This was a beautiful piece of silk that was dyed and hand painted, which was very time consuming and tricky. I found someone who does hand painting, mostly for Broadway productions, and he did a great job.

"We also had beautiful embroidered Chinese boots made for Sun Lok," continues Kaplan, "and we cast a very wide breastplate for him with a dragon

image . . . which at a key moment comes to life, thanks to John Nelson's visual effects. Sun Lok also has very long talons that extend his fingers, which were actually worn in ancient China. And although he doesn't have any jewelry, I had these metal ear tips made which gives him an even eerier look."

Sun Lok's armored skirt comprised more than a thousand hand-pounded leather plates, bound row by row . . . and the costume department fabricated two identical skirts for the character, an enormous amount of handwork by any standards.

Part V

Post*script*

Every movie that's made is a lifetime unto itself, a shared experience that seeps into the memory banks of all its participants, becoming the woof and warp of their consciousnesses. The work was over for the shooting crew, but for Jerry Bruckheimer, Jon Turteltaub, film editor William Goldenberg, composer Trevor Rabin, visual-effects supervisor John Nelson, and the masters of postproduction from Jerry Bruckheimer Films, associate producer Pat Sandston, postproduction supervisor Tami Goldman, and postproduction coordinator Daphne Lambrinou—and so many more technicians and artists—a new stage in the evolution of *The Sorcerer's Apprentice* was just beginning. Editing, scoring, sound effects, visual effects, looping—all had to be accomplished within the one year between wrap in July 2009 and the film's release in July 2010.

But it was all for the cause. Bruckheimer, Turteltaub, Nicolas Cage, and the entire company of *The Sorcerer's Apprentice* were always keenly cognizant of the legacy that had been extended to them in the making of the film. "It's easy to become cynical," notes Turteltaub, "but when you say the name 'Disney,' it touches a part of us that hasn't lost a sense of wanting the world to be filled with humor and support for humanity. We go to the movies because we want the movies to be a better place. It's pretty uncool to be in a good mood these days, but I wish that weren't the case. It's really hard to be an artist who's happy, but a few of us keep trying."

"There will always be a reason to make a movie like *The Sorcerer's Apprentice*," concludes Jerry Bruckheimer. "The appeal of the story is absolutely universal, and resonates with people of every culture and of every age. We all aspire to look inside ourselves and find something better than what we thought was there, whether you're eight or eighty. And we all want to believe that good will always triumph over evil. The technology used to tell the story may change, but the fundamentals are the same. The magic has always been there . . . we just find new ways of creating it."

OPPOSITE: A very satisfied-looking Dave behind the wheel of Balthazar's 1935
Rolls-Royce Phantom, accompanied by Tank (Isabella the Bulldog).

Afterword
Jon Turteltaub

When Nicolas Cage told me he was developing a live-action feature entitled *The Sorcerer's Apprentice* based on the *Fantasia* sequence, my first thought was, "Wow . . . how come no one had thought of that before?" Then when he asked me if I'd be interested in directing it, my first thought was, "If I blow this, everyone at Disney will hate me forever." But taking risks comes with the job and the upside seemed far better than the down. I would have a chance to guide a piece of the Disney legacy and perhaps make a significant contribution to the world of Walt Disney Studios in a way that I never had before. Yay—and yikes!

All of us making the film knew that Disney fans, movie buffs, and film critics would be keeping a particularly close eye on us, lining us up in their sights in the event that we didn't do justice to a great piece of film history. The pressure mounted daily, particularly when dealing with the part of the film that reexamines the confrontation between Apprentice and Broom. In this sequence, we had four options: One, cut the scene out of the film so that no comparisons could ever be made. Two, do a small "wink" at the original short but avoid making it into a big production number. Three, try to do the biggest, best, most high-tech and expensive visual-effects sequence in an attempt to outdo what Walt and his animators did sixty years ago. And four, just focus on telling the overall story of our film and try to incorporate to the best of our ability (and our budget) the themes and ideas explored by Goethe, Dukas, Disney, and others. Choice four was the only way to go.

But what we thought would be limited to that one sequence was actually a feeling of pressure that applied to every sequence. How can we reinvent a classic, paying homage to those brilliant people who came before us, while giving our audience something new and original? The answer is: I DON'T KNOW! All we could do was focus on being true to the characters and story we created. The way things work in Hollywood, even if we're successful and do a great job, people will still find fault and criticize. That's the price of working on big movies. On the other hand, when you work on big movies, people write books on "The Making of . . ." and you get to see your picture and your name in print standing next to some famous people and some really cool sets.

143

OPPOSITE: Father-to-son transmission as Jon Turteltaub shows son Jack one way to light a set with Jay Baruchel looking on approvingly.

ACKNOWLEDGMENTS

When you're a few thousand miles away from home working on a film, those hundred or so people you see on a daily basis become a surrogate family, with all of the highs and lows that go with that relationship. Good days, bad days, shifting moods, companionship, and spats, they see it all, and despite everything, a film company usually emerges from the experience with mutual affection, appreciation, and respect intact. So first and foremost, I'd like to acknowledge my *Sorcerer's Apprentice* family, both cast and crew, and thank them for their endless cooperation and friendship through the long months of shooting. And of course, endless love and thanks to my very own family, Yuko, Miyako, and Kimiko, for tolerating yet another long absence from the absentee husband and father. A deep bow of gratitude to the man who makes it all happen, Jerry Bruckheimer, whose inspiration and kindness cannot be measured, and the entire team at JBF, including Mike Stenson, Chad Oman, Melissa Reid, Pat Sandston, Tami Goldman, and Jill Weiss. Eternal thanks to Jon Turteltaub, for providing me not only with fantastic material to write about day in and out, but also for his wonderfully honest and revealing Afterword for this book. Big thanks to everyone at Walt Disney Studios, including Oren Aviv, Jason Reed, Ryan Stankevich, Christine Cadena, Patrick Skelly, John Sabel, and, especially, Jon Rogers. Appreciation to the staff at Herzog Productions, including Mark Herzog, Joy Lissandrello, Sara O'Reilly, Ed Farmer, and the great Jack Kney. At Disney Editions, my editor, the magnificent Elizabeth Rudnick, was a non-stop source of inspiration, enthusiasm, and collaboration, any writer's dream; also, thanks to Wendy Lefkon, Jennifer Eastwood, Diane Hodges, and this book's marvelous producer and designer, Clark Wakabayashi. Appreciation to Robert ("the Reb") Zuckerman for his luminous photographs. A special shout-out to Hawker, Coogan, and their team for allowing me to share their digs for months on end at the Armory, and to Claire Kirk for helping us put the visual pieces together. Also a great big hello to Lauren Thiessen and Brandon Pride for brightening our set with their indomitable spirits.

This book is dedicated to the memory of our *Sorcerer's Apprentice* colleague Michael Davison, one of the most talented and fiercely dedicated professionals I've ever been privileged and honored to work with. Michael was a voyager, and I'd like to believe that he's still on that journey.

For information address Disney Editions, 114 Fifth Avenue, New York, New York 10011-5690.
VP-Editorial Director: Wendy Lefkon
Editor: Elizabeth Rudnick
Editorial Assistant: Tomas Palacios

Produced by Welcome Enterprises, Inc., 6 West 18th Street, New York, New York 10011
www.welcomebooks.com
Project director/designer: H. Clark Wakabayashi

Photographs by Robert Zuckerman
Additional photographs by Abbot Genser, Myles Aronowitz, and Eric Liebowitz
Page 14 (far right): Photograph by Michael Becker
Page 25: Photograph by Andrew Cooper
Pages 24 & 27: Photographs by Jerry Bruckheimer

The publisher and producer would like to thank the following for their support in the production of this book: Holly Clark, Jennifer Eastwood, Diane Hodges, Richard Jordan, Jon Rogers, Patrick Skelly, and Ed Squair.

Library of Congress Cataloging-in-Publication Data on file.
ISBN 978-1-4231-1706-3
First Edition / 10 9 8 7 6 5 4 3 2 1
Printed in China (G559-1249-8-10032)

Disney.com/SorcerersApprentice